Emma L. Price

Portia's Incredible Journey

Emma L. Price

Portia's Incredible Journey

Emma L. Price

ELP BOOKS®
California

The author proudly acknowledges Dorris S. Woods, Ph.D., RN, CS
for her professional reading of all material relating to diabetes.
Dr. Woods is the author of
Breaking Point Fighting to End America's Teenage Suicide Epidemic!

ISBN-13: 978-0-9841650-0-1
ISBN-10: 0-9841650-0-2
Library of Congress Number: 2009935919

Printed in the United States of America
Second Printing 2010

10 9 8 7 6 5 4 3 2

www.elpbooks.net

Page Layout by Lynn M. Snyder—lmsdesigns4u@hotmail.com

Summary: Portia's diagnosis of type 1 diabetes is only the start of the
many increasingly serious challenges she'll face during this incredible year.

[1. Diabetes—Fiction   2. Bullying—Fiction   3. Friendship—Fiction
4. Family—Fiction   5. Hurricane—Fiction]

Publisher's Note:
This is a work of fiction. Names, characters, places, and incidents
are either products of the author's imagination or are used fictitiously,
and any resemblance to actual persons, living or dead, business
establishments, events, or locales is entirely coincidental.

Please do not attempt any acts that are described within
this book at home or at school.

Dedication

*This book is dedicated to Annie W. Dublin,
Mable R. Burtch (Boylan), and Sara J. Sapp.*

Life isn't about waiting for the storm to pass. It's about learning to dance in the rain.

—Anonymous

Have you ever had to dance in the rain?

"It's gonna hurt. I can't do it!" The words jumped out of my mouth. "I'm too scared."

"You're going to have to learn one day." Mom's voice shot through my mind like an arrow. "We've been talking with you about this for a while. We'll show you so you'll know how by the time school starts."

"We're here to help," Dad said.

"I can't do it." I turned my back to Mom and Dad, crossed my arms, and poked out my lips. "Why do I have to anyway? It'll be—"

"You're not alone," Dad cut in. "We're here for you."

"I know, but those shots hurt." Hot tears stung my cheeks. "I'm not ready."

I ran to my room and slammed the door. Trying to calm down, I held on to the window ledge and stared out the window. Huge, dark clouds pulled my eyes into the center of the storm. I didn't want to be sucked up into it.

How could Mom and Dad do this to me? Why did they tell me *now*, just before my eleventh birthday? Why can't I wait until next year?

I pressed my warm cheek against the cool windowpane, fighting to slow down my fast breathing. Grandma's voice echoed in my mind: "Nature has a way of speaking to us when we are ready to listen."

Exhausted, I plopped down on the foot of my bed.

Mom walked in and sat down next to me.

"Portia, we're trying to make this as easy as possible." She put her arm around my shoulders. "Something else has come up. Dad and I are going through a difficult time too." Her soft voice felt warm, like a hug. "We need you to learn to do this for yourself."

"But Mom, I'm scared."

She gently pushed back the curly brown lock of hair that had fallen over my eye. "I know it's hard, but remember, you're a smart, brave girl. You can do this."

Mom kissed my cheek, got up, and left my room as quietly as she had come in.

I walked to the dresser, opened the sock drawer, pulled out my diary, and gawked at the Mars bar lying between the pink and blue socks. My hand shook as I picked it up, fumbled the wrapper off, and gulped the chocolate down.

Then I opened my diary.

Dear Diary,

Today Mom and Dad told me I had to learn to give myself insulin! They KNOW I'm afraid of needles. What did I do to be cursed with diabetes? I shouldn't eat this candy now, but sweets make me feel better when I'm nervous. And I am SO nervous— I need this chocolate bad! What's worse—I'm so scared!

Mom says something is going on with her and Dad. There's no way it can be as bad as MY problem. I was looking forward to having a great summer. Now everything is messed up. What am I going to do?

—Not Ready

I put my diary back in the drawer, hid the wrapper under other papers in the trash, and glanced out the window. Raindrops beat against the house. I got into bed and turned off the light. In the dark, I tossed and turned, and searched for answers.

How did everything go so wrong so quickly?

Chapter One

It all started when I was nine, the last week of fourth grade. I raised my hand for the third time that hot afternoon.

"Yes, Portia?" Mrs. Levine asked.

"May I be excused to go to the restroom?"

"Portia, when you finish in the restroom, go to the nurse's office." Mrs. Levine sounded mad. "Take this note and give it to Mrs. Bryant, please."

When I opened the door to the nurse's office, the strong smell of rubbing alcohol burned my eyes. I squeezed my nose and waved my hand back and forth in front of my face to chase the stink away.

Three kids waited for Nurse Bryant. A little boy sat in the seat next to her office door, with his knee bent, foot on the chair, holding his left thigh against his red-and-white T-shirt. His knee bled. He sniffed as tears rolled down his cheeks.

Next to him sat Liz Madison, one of the school's worst troublemakers. She was a chubby, red-headed fourth grader.

The chair next to Liz was empty. Mary Ann Walton sat in the next seat over, holding her bruised elbow, leaning as far away from Liz as she could. She looked up at me with sad, sky-blue eyes.

I gave her a quick wave. We used to talk and play together, but after her mom and dad divorced, she didn't talk to me much anymore. She waved back, then looked away.

I signed the sheet on the waiting room table and sat next to Mary Ann. Things are always going wrong for her, and she doesn't even have a grandmother to help her, like I do.

What was Nurse Bryant going to say about me always having to go pee? Oooo! I hated being here. I squeezed my hands.

The nurse's student assistant took the sign-in sheet to her. After the small boy, Liz, and Mary Ann left, the nurse called, "Portia Maddox?"

I trudged into the inner office, handed Nurse Bryant the note, and eased into the chair next to her desk. She wore a white uniform, with a red heart pinned on the collar.

She read the note and looked up at me over her brown-rimmed glasses. "Portia, why do you have to go to the restroom so frequently?"

"I'm always thirsty, and as soon as I drink, I have to use it."

"When did this begin?"

"I think about a month ago."

"How's your appetite?"

"Most of the time I'm hungry and I eat all my food." I looked down at my arms. "And I'm still skinny."

"Do you have to use the bathroom more than two times at night?"

"Sometimes I have to use it three or four times, and then I have to drink more water."

"Do you feel tired and sleepy during the day?"

"Yes, at school and at home."

"I'm sending a note home with you. There may be a bigger problem here, and we want you to be healthy."

"What kinda problem?"

Nurse Bryant glanced at me, then finished writing. She smiled and handed me a long white envelope. "It's too soon to say. Your mom and dad will take care of you. Please give this note to them."

I left the nurse's office with the envelope in my sweaty hand. It weighed a ton. I had no idea that the message inside would change my life forever.

Chapter Two

Liz was waiting for me when I turned the corner to go back to class.

"Yuuuuck!" I groaned under my breath, nearly bumping into her.

"Tell anybody I was in Nurse Bryant's office and you'll be sorry. I'll give you a black eye. I'm no baby!" Liz shouted, the anger boiling in her puffy green eyes. She shook her chubby fist so close to my face that I could smell the sweat on it. "You hear me?"

"I'm not afraid of you, you big bully!" I shouted back, then shoved past her and rushed to class as fast as my feet could carry me.

For the rest of the afternoon, the hands on the classroom clock crept slowly. I counted the seconds to dismissal. What did Nurse Bryant write in that note? I wanted to see what was in it. I knew it was something bad.

Eons later, the bell squealed. I jumped up from my desk,

grabbed my rolling backpack, and dashed for the door.

"Portia, Portia, wait for us!" I heard my friends calling behind me. "Why are you running so fast? We want to walk with you."

I didn't answer.

Rat-a-tat-tat-tat, my backpack bounced on the pavement. I jogged the four blocks home. What was Mom going to say?

I hurried into the house, found Mom, and handed her the rumpled envelope. She opened it carefully. I stood facing her like a statue, except that I was breathing hard, watching her hazel-brown eyes as they moved across the page.

She frowned and whispered, "Oh my goodness. This can't be. Not now!"

"Mom, what's wrong?"

"I need to call Dr. Wells and set up an appointment for tomorrow morning."

"I feel okay," I protested. "I'm just thirsty all the time. I drink water and have to use the restroom."

Mom patted my shoulder. "I know, sweetie, but we need the pediatrician to examine you to see if there's a problem."

That night I gobbled down a pack of chocolate chip cookies from the snack bag in my drawer.

The next day Dr. Wells gave me a complete exam. After she asked a million questions, I took more tests. She pricked my fingers to draw blood at different times during the morning. I couldn't remember ever having my fingers pricked before. It really hurt.

We spent most of the morning at the doctor's office.

"Mrs. Maddox, Portia will have to come back tomorrow for more tests," Dr. Wells said. "I scheduled her as Dr. Thomas's first patient in the morning. It's very important that she doesn't eat any food after midnight tonight. She may drink water. You can bring her a snack, but no food before the tests."

"I understand," Mom said.

We headed home. The troubled look still covered her face. That night I wrote,

Dear Diary,

What's going on with me? Why do I have to go to the restroom so much? Mom is worried. I've never seen such a terrified look on her face. Now I have to go to a special doctor. Will the doctor be able to cure me?

—Worried

We arrived at the clinic early the next morning. I had to miss another day of school. This time, Dad came with us.

The patient exam room was painted all white. It wasn't very big, but there were lots of chairs and a desk stood near the door.

There were a zillion posters of the body all over the walls. A tall gray-haired doctor came in and shook hands with Dad and Mom, then smiled at me.

"Hello, Portia. I'm Dr. Thomas." He held out his hand to me. "I'm a pediatric endocrinologist. I specialize in treating disorders of organs such as the pancreas." His huge hand buried mine.

"Hi," I squeaked.

"Dr. Wells said you're a champion swimmer and that your team won the district championship."

I nodded.

He let go of my hand. "Good for you. I'll just need to get a small sample of blood from your finger. Is that okay?"

"Yes," I murmured under my breath. Sticking my hand out, I closed my eyes.

My empty stomach growled.

Dr. Thomas pricked my finger.

Ouch! I choked back sobs as tears gushed from my eyes and ran down my cheeks. I opened my eyes.

Dr. Thomas handed me a tissue. "I need to check the results of today's tests and review the ones from Dr. Wells." He smiled at me. "Portia, why don't you eat your snack now?"

Mom handed me my snack and asked, "Dr. Thomas, when will we know something?"

"I'll have the results in about ten minutes." Dr. Thomas left the room.

The sandwich took forever to reach my stomach.

A short time later, a nurse called us into the doctor's office. His office had a big window behind his huge desk. The walls were covered with awards and certificates. I sat between Mom and Dad.

"Portia has type 1 diabetes, which is sometimes called juvenile diabetes."

Diabetes? Where had I heard that word before?

"Portia, do you know what the pancreas does?" Dr. Thomas asked.

"I remember learning about it in health. It had something to do with sugar in the blood," I said.

"Yes, the pancreas produces insulin. When it can no longer make insulin, glucose, better known as sugar, builds up in the bloodstream. The sugar rises to an unsafe level in the body." Dr. Thomas got up and leaned on the corner of his desk closer to us. "That's why insulin has to be injected into the body, so glucose can get into the cells, where it is used for energy."

This sounded serious. I dug my nails into the palm of my hand until it turned red.

Dr. Thomas said, "When Portia is constantly thirsty and has to urinate often, those are signs that her body is not properly utilizing glucose."

Did Mom and Dad understand what he was saying?

Dad took my hand. "Dr. Thomas, I have type 2 diabetes. I'm sure Portia doesn't know much about it. I usually take my shots in private. We didn't want to frighten her."

Yes, that's where I heard *diabetes*—Dad!

I swallowed. "I saw you giving yourself a shot one time, and I got really scared."

Dad squeezed my hand. "Yes, Baby Girl, you screamed and cried and begged me not to do it again. I told you I had to get insulin shots because I had diabetes." He looked at Dr. Thomas. "That's when we decided to wait to explain it to her when she got older," Dad told him. "We'll explain it more when we get home."

My heart jumped into my throat, and I squeezed Dad's hand back.

Dr. Thomas walked behind his desk and scribbled on a sheet of paper. "I'm signing the family up for the diabetes education sessions. Will 4 p.m. to 6 p.m. next Tuesday and Wednesday be all right?"

"Yes," Mom answered, and Dad nodded.

I was glad Dr. Thomas didn't say Thursday and Friday. My swim team practiced on those days and I just made team captain. I hope Mom lets me stay on the team.

"Portia, I'm giving you a few pamphlets to read before your first visit."

Dr. Thomas picked up some booklets from his desk and handed them to me. "I know it's a lot for you to understand, but a nurse educator and a dietitian will be available to answer *all* your questions. You'll learn how to test your blood sugar, how to eat right, and how to give yourself insulin injections."

Hold on a minute, I thought. *I don't think so.* I'm scared of taking *any* shots. It was terrible seeing Dad give himself one.

"There's nothing to worry about, young lady. There are many new devices to make injections less painful. In fact, a new insulin pump is in the final stages of being tested. We'll take good care of you," he promised, extending his hand to me.

I took it, my legs feeling wobbly.

"I'll be checking very closely the next few weeks to see how you're doing. Then we'll set up exams every three months or so. Don't hesitate to call if questions come up. Do you have any now?"

Not trusting my voice, I shook my head.

So began my life as a soon-to-be-ten-year-old kid with diabetes.

Chapter Three

After Mom and I completed the diabetes sessions, the nurse gave me a purple glucose meter, and the dietitian made up a thirty-day food plan to help Mom with my meals.

Then the routine began. At least four times a day, Mom would tell me it was time to check my blood sugar. I tried to be brave when she pricked my finger and the blood oozed out, but I wasn't. I sobbed.

"It's important to record your blood sugar levels in the daily log," Mom said. "We have to take it to Dr. Thomas on your next visit."

Whenever Mom and Dad started to give me insulin shots, which I had to take two times a day, I would scream, "Ouch! It hurts!"

"Try to settle down," Mom said one time, rubbing my shoulders. "Take deep breaths, relax, and it won't hurt so much."

"I can't!" Tears rolled down my face. "I don't know how."

I shut my eyes tight. I didn't want to see the needle. If I couldn't see it, maybe the shots wouldn't hurt so badly.

Mom pulled me close to her. "It'll get a little easier as time passes."

I didn't believe those horrible shots would ever hurt any less.

"Portia," Dad said. I knew he was serious because he *never* called me by my name. "Your mom and I don't like causing you pain. I know these shots hurt. We're doing everything we can to make it easier for you. You'll get used to them and the routine."

But I didn't get used to the routine or the shots. I was nervous, and I still sneaked goodies out of my bag.

A few days later, Mom checked my log. "I don't understand why the past few readings show your blood sugar is on the high side. I'm going to call the doctor and ask what he thinks is happening."

"No, Mom," I begged. "I'm just nervous from taking those shots. I don't want to go back to the doctor. Test my blood sugar later today—please."

I didn't eat any more candy that day. I *had* to stick to my meal plan or I'd have to see the doctor, and he'd know I'd been sneaking junk foods. Mom tested my blood sugar later, and it was moving closer to my target level. I worked hard to keep it there.

A few weeks before Thanksgiving, I started paying attention when Mom tested me.

Soon, no more sobbing.

In late December, I asked, "Mom, can I try to test myself?"

She smiled. "Sure, wash your hands with warm, soapy water and dry them."

I washed my hands.

"Now take the glucose meter and the strip. Remember you want to prick the side of your finger in the first joint."

I took the very fine, sharp disposable needle, and pricked the side of my finger. A drop of blood oozed out. I placed it on the strip and inserted the strip into the glucose meter. My blood sugar was normal.

Mom said, "Great job, Portia! I'm proud of you."

"I *can* do it myself."

Mom watched me for three or four days to make sure I was testing correctly, then she trusted me to do my own testing. Now, six months since the doctor had diagnosed me, I knew the routine. The only thing I still couldn't do was give myself shots. But Mom kept finding ways for me to practice.

She gave me an orange in the kitchen one afternoon. "This'll help you get used to holding the needle and giving yourself shots." She handed me a needle filled with water. "Take the needle and inject the water into the orange. This is good practice for you and you'll see it's really easy. Give it a try."

I shook my head. "No, it's not easy. I don't think I'll ever be ready to give myself shots." I stuck the needle in the orange. "If I did, it'd hurt more than it already does. I don't want any more pain."

Mom sighed. "One day you'll have to."

I was glad my diabetes was under control. I was full of energy and didn't have to run to the restroom all the time, especially after drinking water. I had even stopped sneaking sweets.

"I don't like getting the shots and they still hurt," I told Mom, "but now I'm used to them, and I know what to expect. I'm learning how to relax a little more."

"Yes, I noticed you're talking now while getting your insulin and that's a good sign."

Mom's "good sign" was the beginning of a big, scary change in my life.

Chapter Four

"Portia, come here, please," Mom called a few weeks before my eleventh birthday.

I hurried to the kitchen where Mom and Dad waited, then stopped abruptly when I saw the look on their faces.

"Your mom and I want to talk to you," Dad said. "Everything's all right. You're not in any trouble."

"Wheew!" I plunked down in a chair. The seat seemed harder than usual.

"Portia," Mom began, "now that you're getting ready to go to middle school, your dad and I decided it's time for you to learn how to give yourself shots. We've been using the injector pen instead of the needle for the past month, so this should make it easier for you."

I shifted. My eyes focused on the clock over the kitchen sink.

"We discussed it with Dr. Thomas," Dad added. "We think you're mature enough to take charge."

"Oooo," I moaned. I placed both hands on the arm of my chair and rearranged my bottom in it.

"You've been doing a good job with your testing, but it's time for you to learn to do it all," Mom said. "We can't always be with you when you need insulin." Then she smiled and said, "You know we can't go to college with you."

My head throbbed.

"You said you wanted to go to camp for a week. You don't want to be the only one who doesn't know how to give herself insulin, do you?" Dad asked.

"Nooo, but I'm scared," I said, moving my finger around the curve of the table.

Dad and Mom watched me without speaking. It seemed that the hands on the clock stopped moving.

Mom sat with her shoulders squared and her face firmly fixed. Finally, she said, "It's time for you to learn."

I knew then that neither Mom nor Dad was going to give in. My tongue turned to lead. I wished Grandma were here. She would have helped me.

My parents' words sunk into my brain and my tongue finally came back to life. "I can't give myself shots! How can you ask me? You know I'm scared. Why can't I wait until next year? Then I'll be ready to learn."

No response from them. No sounds. No yelling. Hot tears

ran down my cheeks. Dad moved his chair closer to Mom's, and both remained still, their eyes fixed on me—sadness and disappointment covered their faces.

But I couldn't think of them. My hands shook. What about me? What about my pain? I ran my finger back and forth over my bracelet.

Dad knew I expected him to come to my rescue. He'd always been on my side.

"You're growing into a fine young lady. You act older than your years. You'll do just fine and we'll help as long as you need us," Dad said with a "You *have* to do this" look on his face.

I jumped up from the chair and screamed, "Neither one of you is listening to me! I'm not ready. I'll never forgive you if you make me do it. I've done everything else for myself. Why can't you help me just a little longer? Please. Pleeease."

I didn't wait for an answer. I ran to my room. Now standing, looking out my window, their words echoed in my head.

Chapter Five

"Portia?" Mom called. "Sarah's on the phone."

Uggh! That's all I needed. Sarah is always acting silly and telling jokes. I don't need any clowning around or—well, maybe she could help me.

Sarah is my cousin. Her mother is Dad's sister. Sarah is six months younger than I am. We have the same grayish hazel eyes and the same shade of amber skin, like my father. Our parents say we look more like sisters than cousins.

I ran to the kitchen and picked up the phone.

"Hi, Sarah."

"Hi, kiddo. Aunt Grace said it would be all right if I came to spend two weeks with you before you go to camp. Is that okay?"

"Yeah! I'm mad and need to talk to you. I don't know how I'm going to make it through the summer. Things are so awful."

"What's the matter?"

"I'll tell you when you get here. Mom and Dad told me I *have* to do something."

"Parents always tell us what we have to do," Sarah said.

"But this is terrible! You won't believe—" A beep interrupted me.

"Sorry, Sarah, another call is coming in. I'll tell you when you get here." I clicked over to the caller, but whoever it was hung up and the line went dead. Funny, that's the third time this week this has happened to me.

I hurried to the living room and found Mom and Dad sitting at opposite ends of the sofa. A chill shot through me. Had they been arguing?

"Sarah's coming to spend two weeks with us this summer!" I said.

"Good," Mom said. "Last summer you didn't get to spend any time with her."

Dad didn't say anything. I turned and walked back to my room.

Sarah was coming. I would have someone who'd listen to *my* side of the story.

Five years ago, Aunt Leslie, Uncle Frank, and Sarah moved to Selma, which is about fifty miles from where we live in Charlottesville. Every summer since then, we spent two weeks together either at my house or at hers, but not last year. We visited them on Thanksgiving, and they came to our house on New Year's Day.

Should I tell Sarah I have diabetes? I didn't want her feeling sorry for me. That's why I hadn't told her yet and besides, we hadn't seen each other much.

Later that night when I got up to go to the kitchen, I heard Dad say, "I love you too, Baby Girl. Bye." He hung up the phone.

I just stood there. "Daddy, who were you talking to?" Tears came into my eyes, and my voice quivered. "You always call *me* Baby Girl."

Dad put his arms around me and hugged me.

"Don't worry. You're still my Baby Girl."

"But, Daddy," I said, sniffing. "Who were you talking to?"

"Portia, you're tired and it's been a long day—off to bed with you." He gave me a goodnight hug and pushed me toward my room. I know he was still hiding something from me. Now I had one more thing to worry about.

The next morning I had to practice with my swimming team. My head ached. Too much was happening. When Mom gave me my shot, I turned my head, closed my eyes, and groaned. This one seemed to hurt more than ever.

She didn't say anything about our talk last evening and I didn't say anything about Dad on the phone.

I tried to eat breakfast, but nothing would go down. Finally, I hid it in the trash under some papers so Mom wouldn't see it. I didn't want her getting on my case again.

Later that morning, when Mom drove me to the pool, it was still sprinkling.

"I'll be back in an hour to pick you up. Sorry we're running late. Enjoy your practice," Mom said, hugging me. "Do you have your kit?"

"Yes. See you later, Mom."

All the kids and Coach Susan were standing near the pool.

"Hi, Portia," Dejah, my swimming buddy and friend, called out. "Hurry and get ready." Her glassy brown eyes sparkled as she bounced up and down.

"Hello, Portia." Coach Susan waved. "Quick, hurry!"

I put my diabetes kit in the storage bin where the other two kids with diabetes keep their kits and ran to the locker area to change into my swimsuit.

"Okay, captains, get your teams practicing," Coach Susan ordered. "We have an important competition at Westlake School next Saturday. Start your team with laps."

After practicing with my team through the first set of laps, I forgot all about giving myself shots. The water had relaxed me.

"Enjoying yourself, huh?" Dejah laughed. "I see you smiling."

"Yeah. I love the water. I feel good when I'm in it."

On the last lap, about a foot from the edge of the pool, I felt like something was pulling me to the bottom.

"Help!" I yelled. "Something's pulling me!"

My heart raced. My legs grew heavy. I tried to reach for the ledge of the pool, but my arms refused to move.

"Get me out!" I pushed hard to force the words.

The water felt like mud, sucking me under.

"Portia! Portia! What's wrong? Are you okay?" I heard sluggish, muffled sounds from far away.

"Help me get her out of the water!" a voice ordered.

I looked up and saw a blurred vision of Jenny, the lifeguard.

"Call 9-1-1. I'm calling her mom," another voice murmured from far away.

I slurred, "Dooon't caaall Mooooom."

"I have her kit," Dejah cried. "Here! Here!"

Coach Susan and Jenny sat me up. Dejah held the juice to my mouth.

"Did you take your morning shot and eat your breakfast?" Coach Rick asked.

Coach Susan bent over me. "Your mom is two blocks away

and the paramedics are on the way."

The orange juice was slowly working.

"I'll be okay." My tongue was still a little heavy.

The siren blasted into the pool area. All the kids crowded around for a look.

Feeling slowly came back into my body. My vision cleared up.

A few seconds later, the doors to the pool house swung open and a team of paramedics and Mom raced in together.

"Take another sip." Coach Susan tipped the juice carton to my lips.

"Is Portia all right?" Mom yelled. "What happened?"

Mom rubbed my arm. Her hand felt warm like the early morning sun.

"Portia's blood sugar is low," Jenny said. "She was shaking and had trouble speaking."

"Signs of an insulin reaction," said Coach Rick.

"How do you feel, honey?" Mom looked into my eyes and touched my cheeks.

"Is everything under control?" one of the paramedics asked.

"Yes, she just gave us a little scare. This has happened a few times before with other students," Coach Rick said, "and it sure happened to me when I was young."

"I'm going to take her blood sugar," said the paramedic as he knelt beside me.

"Thank you," Mom said.

The paramedic tested me. "It's still low."

"Portia, finish your juice," Mom said. "What happened?" she asked again.

I tried to sit up, but settled for propping myself up on my elbows.

"I didn't eat breakfast this morning. I tried, but it wouldn't go down. I was upset from last night. I know better now."

Boy, this is embarrassing! All the kids are staring at me. *Zap me out of here, somebody!*

"Do you need us anymore, ma'am?" a paramedic asked Mom.

"No, I know what to do," Mom assured him. "I'll take her home. We'll test her in about fifteen minutes to be sure her sugar is back to normal. If I need to, I'll take her to the hospital. Thank you so much."

Coach Rick pulled me to my feet. He didn't let go until I could stand up straight and take a few steps.

"Dejah, go with Portia to the locker area and help her get dressed," Coach Susan said. "Don't forget your kit, Portia."

"You're a good friend," I said as we walked to the lockers. Dejah, as usual, bounced every step as she walked. She took my hand, smiled, and gave me a piece of hard candy from my kit.

On the way home, Mom said, "You know the insulin needs something to work on. Your blood sugar will get low when you get a shot and don't eat. You shouldn't take chances like that."

"Yes, Mom, I know now." I took a sip of juice. "I promise not to let it happen again."

Back home, I went to my room and looked in the mirror. My pale amber skin looked lifeless, like a ghost.

I pulled out my diary.

Dear Diary,

Today was a terrible day! I had my first insulin reaction. I could have drowned. I've never been so scared in my life. I was so ashamed. Even though the kids know I have diabetes, it was still embarrassing. I want to help Mom and Dad with my shots, but I'm not ready. I'm scared. What can I do?

—Still Scared

I tested my blood sugar. It was near normal and I was feeling okay.

"Portia, lunch is ready," Mom called.

It was hard swallowing, but I forced the hot dog and milk

down. I didn't want that horrible feeling I had at the pool to come back. I never wanted to go through that again.

Chapter Six

At last, the Friday evening for Sarah's visit came. Every time I heard a car go by, I ran to the window. The rain kept falling, splashing in the street. Dad and Mom watched television without speaking to one another.

What's wrong with them? Were they mad at each other? I was doing all the talking.

"Mom, why's it taking them so long? Do you think Uncle Frank was driving too fast and got into an accident again?"

"I don't know, dear," Mom said and shook her head. "We just have to be patient until they get here." She got up and went to the kitchen. I followed her.

Her eyes were red. "Mom, what's wrong? Are you crying?"

She placed her arm around my shoulders. "No, Portia. I didn't sleep well last night." She patted my shoulder. "Let's go back in the den and wait for your cousin."

I took her hand. "I want you and Dad to be happy. It's no fun in this house anymore."

Mom squeezed my hand. "Things will get better soon."

Finally, Uncle Frank pulled his car into our driveway.

"Yeaaah!" I shouted. "Sarah's here!" I rushed to open the door.

Sarah ran up the steps. The wind blew her long hair over her wet face.

"It's been forever!" I said and we reached for each other.

"Hello, Aunt Grace and Uncle Russell," Sarah said to my parents.

I hugged and kissed her mom and dad.

Giggling, Sarah and I grabbed each other's hands and skipped to my room.

After Sarah's parents left, we dashed to the kitchen. "Sarah, I'm going to make a tortilla with melted cheese. Do you want one?"

"Yes, and after I finish, I'm going to have a cookie." She sounded defiant.

What's wrong with her? Why was she using that tone? She's always been the jolly one.

"Do you want a cookie, too?" she asked.

"No thanks." Tomorrow I would tell her my problem.

After we finished eating, Sarah and I went back to my room. We got ready for bed. As usual, she had a lot of new jokes. I laughed so much, my stomach ached. We played Scrabble, acted silly, and talked late into the night. That is until Mom called, "Hey, you two better stop all that noise and get to sleep so you can get up and go to the mall tomorrow morning."

We put our heads under the covers, lowered our voices, and continued acting silly. Finally, exhausted, we fell asleep.

When the alarm woke me up at seven o'clock the next morning, Sarah wasn't in bed. I heard her in the bathroom. I waited for a long time, but she didn't come out.

I couldn't take it any longer. I called, "Sarah, do you need anything?"

"No, I'm okay. Don't come in!" she yelled. "I'll be out in a sec. I have to do something." A few minutes later, she opened the door.

"What do you have to do so early in the morning?"

"I had to take my insulin shot," she moaned.

My mouth popped open. I couldn't believe my ears. "You have diabetes?"

"Yeah! It's a bore. I *hate* it and when I go on sleepovers, it's even worse!" An angry frown crinkled her forehead.

"Eerie!"

"What do you mean?" Sarah asked.

"'Cause I have it too!"

"You do?"

"Yes," I groaned.

"Oh my goodness! We *are* alike!" Sarah cried. "Last year, I had to start taking insulin. That's why I didn't come to spend time with you last summer. I didn't want to tell you. I've been giving myself injections for the past month."

"You know how to give yourself shots? That's what Mom and Dad are trying to get me to do!"

"It's not so bad, but the routine sucks—test your blood sugar, take your shot, eat your meals and snacks, run and play, over and over." Sarah threw up both hands. "Oooo! I hate it! I can't eat like my friends. If they want a soda, they just buy one and drink it. I have to check my blood sugar first to see if I can drink one too."

"I know, but the routine isn't my problem. I'm afraid of giving myself shots."

"I felt the same way. I didn't want to do it either. Now I'm used to the shots. They don't hurt too bad. I hate not being able to eat anything I like when I want it, and I hate the routine." She rolled her eyes. "If I have to take insulin, why can't I eat anything I like when I want to?"

"I don't understand a lot about diabetes, but we have to be careful."

"Yeah! Yeah! I know. I've heard it a kazillion times. I had to promise Mom and Dad I'd take my shots, and not eat a lot of junk or skip meals, or they weren't going to let me stay with you." She looked down at her hands. "Last month I spent three days in the hospital because I didn't take my shots when I spent two nights at Becky's. My blood sugar went way high. It scared us to death. I promised Mom and Dad I would never do that again."

"I had a bad thing happen too, at the swimming pool just last week, and I learned my lesson," I said. "Let's get ready for breakfast."

"Yeah! Bacon smells good." She gave me a butt bump. We laughed.

In the kitchen, Mom gave me my shot.

"Sarah has diabetes and knows how to give herself insulin," I told Mom.

"Yes, her mom said she was good at giving herself shots."

Mom *knew* Sarah had diabetes?

She smiled. "Pretty soon you'll know how, too."

A shiver of fear shot through my body.

"Are you two ready to go shopping?" Mom asked after we'd finished eating. We jumped up and ran to the garage.

At the mall, I bought some flip-flops, a swimsuit, and a swim cap to take to camp. And I just *had* to buy another gold charm for the bracelet Dad gave me. Sarah spent her money on a Monopoly game, M&Ms, and nacho cheese chips.

I wondered if I should tell Mom, but I remembered how I

felt when I used to sneak junk food and sweets. I didn't want to get Sarah into trouble.

Back home, at lunch, Mom said, "Sarah, I'm so glad you're here. Portia is having a difficult time dealing with the idea of giving herself shots. When your mom told me how well you were doing, I knew you'd be the one to help her."

"Aunt Grace, I told Portia I'd help her, and she said she wanted me to."

Mom smiled and patted her hand.

After lunch, Sarah and I went outside to jump rope.

"Portia, don't you ever cheat and eat something you want that you're not supposed to?" Sarah asked.

"Sometimes. But I'm getting better at not cheating."

"I wish I could be as good as you sticking to my routine. I hate it when I'm in the middle of something and have to stop and test."

"It wasn't always like this with me. I used to sneak sweets. We can help each other," I said. "I'll help you plan ways to stick to your routine, and maybe you can help me get over the fear of giving myself shots."

Sarah shrugged. "Cool."

Later that afternoon, Sarah and I called her mom to ask questions about the two-week meal plan she'd sent with her.

"I'm glad Sarah is visiting you," Aunt Leslie said. "We were hoping she'd see how well you're doing sticking to your routine, and she'd try to do the same. We had such a scare last month!"

We spent the next day finding ways to solve Sarah's problem. First, we asked Mom for suggestions.

"It might be best to write down what you two have in common with your diabetes care. Start from there," Mom told us.

Next, we took out Sarah's meal plan. "Let's see where we can plan a sweet for you," I said. "You might have to test more and take extra insulin."

Sarah took a chocolate chip cookie out of her bag. "I need this cookie." She held it up in the air and turned it over in her hand, "so I can concentrate." We both giggled.

"Let's see where we can start," I said.

Sarah grabbed a pen and marked a big red X through most of her meals. We looked at each other, let out a loud laugh, and rolled over on the floor.

Finally, we got serious. Mom said to see what we have in common. "We get up at the same time, so we can test then. How does that sound?"

"Good thinking," Sarah said. "I have to take two shots a day just like you and eat three meals and three snacks, too."

"How many times do you test?" I asked.

"Supposed to test at least four times a day."

"Me too," I said. "This is great. We can start testing

together tomorrow."

"Okay, guess I can give it a try."

The next morning at breakfast, Sarah and I laid out our plan for Mom to look over.

"This is great! You two have put your heads together and come up with a wonderful plan. I'm so proud of you."

Sarah and I followed the plan the next few days, and she stuck to the routine.

Three nights later, I wrote.

Dear Diary,

Sarah is doing good sticking to the routine. She hasn't sneaked junk food once. Now I need to get enough courage to give myself a shot. I'm going to keep my eyes open to see how Mom does it when she gives me insulin. I can't let them down. I have to start being brave. Sarah is younger than I am and she can do it. I can do it too.

—Ready to Try

The next day I started paying attention when Mom gave me my shots. I kept my eyes open and I asked a lot of questions. I watched closely when Sarah gave herself shots.

"Portia, relax your arm like this, so the shot won't hurt so much," Sarah said, showing me what to do. "When you get a shot in the behind, turn your toes inward. Mom said that way you won't tense up your bottom, and the shot won't hurt!" We giggled and fell against the wall.

"Now," Sarah said, "it's your turn. Let's get the injector pen!"

I froze.

"Come on. You can't keep putting it off forever," Sarah said.

"I know. I'll try tomorrow."

Could I bring myself to be as brave as Sarah? Did I have the courage to stick a needle in my thigh?

Chapter Seven

On Monday morning, in a shaky voice, I announced, "Today's the day. I'm ready to give myself a shot."

"Good for you!" Mom cheered, "and just in time before breakfast."

"Yeah!" Sarah said and playfully bumped against me.

Mom placed the insulin pen, cotton balls, and alcohol on the table.

My heart thumped so loud I thought it would pop out of my chest.

The tiny disposable needle on the end of the insulin pen drew my focus. The hardest part would be sticking the needle into my thigh.

I cringed.

My head throbbed. My eyes blurred, and my body began to shake.

"I *gotta* do this," I whispered to myself. "I have to relax. Relax. Relax."

"First," Mom said with her soft voice, "take the hand sanitizer and clean your hands."

I opened the small bottle she handed me and poured a few drops of the liquid sanitizer on the palms of my hands. I quickly rubbed my hands together and wiped them with a paper towel.

A new cartridge was inside the insulin pen. I picked up the pen and did as Mom had shown me. The right dose of insulin was in the pen.

"Now, put some alcohol on a cotton ball and clean the area on your thigh where you're going to give yourself the shot."

I slowly wiped the spot and let it dry.

She smiled.

Shaking, I sat down, wishing it were over. Sweat popped out on my arms and dripped down to my hands.

"You're doing a great job!" Mom encouraged. "Now, take the insulin pen and hold it like this." She showed me.

My sweaty hand shook. I had to hold the pen in my right hand at a slight angle. I felt Mom's hand on top of mine.

Thanks, Mom. I need your help!

She leaned closer. "Now with your left hand, gently pinch a bit of your skin between your thumb and fingers."

Out of the corner of my eye, I saw Sarah with her fingers crossed. I pinched my skin.

"That's it! Take the pen and quickly insert the needle into your thigh."

I did what Mom said while my heart skipped, then beat faster and faster. Sweat ran down my forehead.

"Great! Now, let go of your skin. Good. Slowly push the blunt end of the pen down so all the insulin will come out. Great job." She removed her hand.

I froze.

"Portia," Mom said, "pull the needle out at the same angle you put it in."

"I'm scared. I can't! "

"Yes, you can," Sarah shouted.

Squinting, I pulled the needle out. "Wheew!"

I sat motionless for a second, breathing hard. Surprise! No pain!

"Good!" Mom said and rubbed my hand.

My legs wobbled as I walked over to the counter and ejected the needle from the pen. Then I put the used cotton balls into the red disposable container.

"Yes!" I pulled my arms down in a victory sweep. "It didn't hurt at all."

Making a soundless clapping motion with her hands, Sarah flashed a big grin.

"Nice going, kiddo. The next time will be easier."

"I'm still shaking." I held out my hands.

"You did a terrific job," Mom said. "Wait till your father gets home and you can tell him the good news."

"Mom, can Sarah and I cook our breakfast this morning?"

"I don't see why not. You've earned it." She winked at me and left the kitchen.

Sarah grabbed me around the neck. "I know how you feel."

"I'm so glad you're here with me. I don't know if I could've done it without you. You're the best." I gave Sarah a big hug.

She grinned. "So are you," she said and gave me one of her famous butt bumps.

"After breakfast, let's ask Mom if we can go to the park and skate. Some of my friends will be there, and she told me to invite a few of them to my birthday party this Saturday."

That evening when Dad got home, he gave me a big smile. "Always knew you'd do a great job, Baby Girl." He patted the top of my head.

"Daddy, I'm sorry for the way I acted about the shots. I was so scared."

"We love you and know how hard this is for you."

He grinned and gave me a thumbs-up every time he saw me that night.

Mom gave me one of the best birthday parties ever. I had a small piece of cake and a big scoop of chocolate ice cream.

Dejah and my swim team came. They put their money together and bought me a pair of gold earrings. Sarah gave me a musical jewelry box.

All my friends seemed to love Sarah and all her corny jokes. They made her feel like she was one of the gang. Turning eleven is special, and it was even more special because I was so happy.

Sarah had accepted her routine and now I finally had the nerve to give myself shots. She and I took our shots at the same time. We made up code letters for times to test our blood sugar or get shots. One of us would say, "It's 'T' time," for a blood sugar test, or "it's 'S' time, for shots." During the rest of Sarah's visit, I learned to inject the insulin in my arms, stomach, and thighs.

Too soon, it was time for Sarah to go home.

"I promise to write you every week and call you too," I told her. "I'll still need your help."

Sarah giggled. "Thanks. I'll need your help too. You're the best cousin anyone could ever have!" We butt bumped.

Sarah grabbed me and whispered, "T and S time."

Neither of us wanted our visit to end, but Sarah had to go. I stood at the door, waving, smiling, and missing her already.

That night, alone in my room, I thought about how much I loved my parents. I stood at the window looking at the stars. When had the rain stopped? The sky was clear, a heavenly light blue, lit by a golden moon. Every star stood proud, daring a cloud to show its head.

I was overjoyed to know how to give myself insulin.

While I pulled out my bags to start packing for camp, Mom came to my room.

"Need any help?"

"Yes, I'm not sure what to take." I studied the packing list in the camp brochure.

"You know there will be rocks and pebbles on the trails at camp, and you need protection for your feet," Mom said. "So you *must* take your hiking boots," she insisted.

"Okay, but I'm wearing my sneakers until we get there."

After we finished packing, Mom said good night, and I took my diary from the nightstand.

Dear Diary,

The past months have been an awful time for me. When my parents told me I had to learn to give myself shots, I freaked out! I wasn't ready. I knew I couldn't do it. The first time I gave myself a shot, I was grateful Mom and Sarah were there to help me. I shook all over. Somehow, I got through it. The next times were a little easier. Now, it's better.

I feel so grown up. When Grandma Ruth said a long time ago, "The stars shine brightest after a storm," I didn't understand. Now, I do. Yes, there was a storm, but now the storm is over—life is great. Happy birthday to me, I'm eleven years old!

—Safely Out of the Storm

I walked to the window, looked toward the sky, and whispered, "Thank you." I'm ready for camp. Nothing can spoil this week.

Chapter Eight

"FriendShip Camp, here I come!" I yelled, tossing my tote bag in the back seat. "Yeaaah! I'm gonna have fun. I can hardly wait!" I slid in next to the bag and closed my door.

"I'm glad the nurse recommended this camp," Mom said. "She said it's one of the best in the state for children with diabetes." Mom got into the front seat and smiled back at me, eyeing my new yellow and brown camp shirt. "That T-shirt looks good on you."

Dad plunked my duffel bag into the trunk, closed it, and then got in the car.

"Yes," I looked down at my shirt. "And it fits too."

"So what are you most looking forward to doing?" Dad asked, backing the car out of the driveway. "I know you're going to do a lot of swimming."

"Yes, I am."

"Maybe Portia wants to try something new. What about horseback riding?" Mom asked.

"I've never been on a horse before." I shrugged. "But I'm going to give it a try."

"That's my 'give-it-a-try-girl'!" Dad chuckled.

We drove for the next hour, and neither Mom nor Dad spoke to one another. That was strange. They always talked quietly in the front seat when we rode in the car. Sometimes we'd even sing. What was going on? Something was wrong.

My mind flashed back to seeing Mom sad and crying. An uneasy feeling crept into my stomach.

Shaking the memories, I asked, "How much longer, Daddy?"

"Not much longer."

The two-hour drive seemed like forever.

The hilly road, draped by tall pines and big leafy bushes, snaked up as we drove toward the mountains. Finally, Dad made a turn onto a dirt road. The steep hills became flatter and rolled out into a huge valley.

"Baby Girl," Dad called. "We're close to the camp."

The seat belt pulled tightly against my body, like it was trying to stop me from seeing. I stretched my neck so I could get a better look. The camp was nestled at the foot of the mountains, surrounded by millions of tall trees.

The golden sun hung just above the hills. A zillion red, white, and blue balloons filled the sky. Just like magic, we were in another world. Music greeted us as we drove through the gate, and my dream of a fun week returned.

Dad drove beneath the big sign, "Welcome to FriendShip Camp."

The main cabin stood off to the right, flags waving from the rooftop. Girls and boys with their families and bags waited in lines to be assigned to cabins.

We pulled into a big field, marked with yellow flags, to the left of the main cabin. "Please pull your car all the way to the front, sir," instructed a boy wearing a camp hat, T-shirt, and yellow armband.

Dad parked the car and I grabbed my tote bag. When we got out, a warm gust of air brushed my face. I lifted my arms, threw my head back, and yelled, "It's super being out here in the wide open space. I looove it! This is going to be an awesome week."

"Well," Dad said, smiling, "let's get in line so you can start your awesome week."

He grabbed my bag out of the trunk, and we walked to the end of the line. When we reached the registration table, I was assigned to cabin four.

"It's just up the trail," said the lady at the table, pointing to a rocky path that led to twelve cabins. "Your counselor will show you the way. Wendy, this is Portia and her parents. Please escort them to cabin four."

A girl about sixteen, wearing a safari suit, hiking boots, and a cap with her long black ponytail hanging out, gave me a quick wave.

I was glad I'd brought my hiking boots. I didn't want to bring them, even though the brochures listed them as a must-have. I wanted to bring only my sneakers. Mom even told me to bring two pairs of boots, the high tops, and the low cuts. She said that way I could change off if I wanted.

"Hi, Portia," Wendy said. "Welcome to FSC. I'll take you and your parents to our cabin."

We followed her to cabin four, next to the tennis court. A flagpole stood nearby.

Wendy opened the door. "There are two cots left. They're the ones with the FriendShip caps on them. Which one do you want?"

There were four cots in one row and three in the other. Each had its own chest of drawers and a footlocker, marked with the same number. Wendy's was the last cot in the row of four. On her footlocker was the word "Counselor."

A small refrigerator stood between two cabinets in the corner. A door led to the bathroom and shower area on the opposite side.

"I'll take that one." I pointed to the one next to the last. I don't like being the last of anything.

Now, there was only one cot left, next to me at the end.

"This is awesome! We all have our own space," I said. "And it smells so fresh in here."

The floor shined. The squeaky-clean cabin smelled like the pines. Long windows ran the length of the knotty pine walls, above the cots on both sides of the cabin.

"Portia, don't forget to follow your schedule of testing and shots," Mom said. "Make sure you follow the rules and try to have someone with you when you go out of the cabin."

"Don't worry," Wendy assured Mom. "Campers are asked to be in sight of each other when they walk around camp. They should stay close to the main grounds. We'll go over the rules. I sleep in the cabin with the girls. I know when they're to test and get their insulin shots. Counselors are trained and certified before they are assigned to a cabin. This is my second year. I used to be a camper here, too."

"That's reassuring," Mom said.

"Portia, while your parents are saying goodbye," Wendy said, "I'm going to go pick up the last girl. It was nice meeting you, Mr. and Mrs. Maddox."

While Mom and Dad helped me get settled and unpacked, two girls entered the cabin and stood by the door.

"Your cabin buddies are here, so we'll leave now," Mom said.

"Call us if you need to, Baby Girl," Dad said. "They have your insulin, and remember, the doctor and the nurse are on duty all the time."

"Yes, Daddy, I will." I tried not to show how nervous I was, knowing my parents expected me to be brave. I hugged and kissed both of them.

"Don't worry. I'll take good care of myself," I said.

They said hello to the girls and left.

"Hi," the girl with long blonde hair said, smiling at me. "I'm Rebekah and this is Sophie the Terrific. We've been walking around camp. There are lots of things to do."

When Rebekah stopped talking, my eyes moved to Sophie. Her face was round and her velvet black hair cut to fit the shape of her small face. She wore black-rimmed glasses. She was cute and looked very young.

"Why do you call her 'The Terrific'?"

Rebekah started to open her mouth.

"Hey!" Sophie said. "You're sleeping next to me. Terrrrific!"

Rebekah and I giggled.

I walked over to them. "My name is Portia. When I finish unpacking, I want to come with you."

"We'll wait for you outside on the steps," Rebekah said.

"Awesome," I said.

I unpacked as fast as I could. Just as I was finishing, Rebekah called out, "Portia, Wendy is coming with the last girl. We'll meet you under the flagpole."

"Okay, I'll be out in a sec. I need to use the restroom."

Two seconds later, I heard the cabin door open and then a scream. "I don't want to stay here! Don't leave me here. I won't stay."

Walking out of the restroom, I thought that this must be her first time staying away from home. I'll say something to try to help calm her down. When I looked up, our eyes locked. She stopped yelling. It was the bully from my school, Liz Madison.

Oh, no! Of all the kids at camp, why was she assigned to *my* cabin?

"Elizabeth, do you know this young lady?" Liz's mom asked. "Are you two friends?"

Liz rolled her eyes. "She goes to my school and is such a wimp!"

Liz's mom shook her head. "That's not nice. Apologize now, Elizabeth."

"Sorry."

"That's okay," I said, determined to try again. "When you finish unpacking, do you want to go—"

"No!" Liz cut in. "I'm not gonna stay here. I don't wanna be here with a bunch of babies!"

"Elizabeth needs time to get used to the place." Her mom smiled at me apologetically. "Go with your friends. She'll be here when you get back."

Liz spun around, opened her duffel bag, and threw all of her clothes on the floor.

I ran out the door, my feet barely touching the ground. Liz has diabetes. I couldn't believe it. No way. I wondered if that was why she had been in the nurse's office last year. She had to test her blood sugar and get shots just like the rest of us.

Will my dream of an exciting week turn out to be a nightmare?

Chapter Nine

"What took you so long?" Rebekah huffed.

"I had to finish putting my things away. You'll never guess who is sleeping in the cot next to me."

"Who?" Rebekah and Sophie asked at the same time.

"My least favorite person in the whole wide world, a big troublemaker from my school."

"No way!" Rebekah said.

"Yes, and she got mad—threw all her clothes on the floor!"

"Then what happened?" Sophie asked.

"Is that a map of the camp?" I leaned closer, trying to change the subject. I didn't want to talk about Liz.

"Yes. It shows all the sites and activities." Rebekah held it up.

Several boys raced by. One yelled, "Hey, let's go to the lake for a boat ride!"

"Come on!" another boy called out. "Let's go."

"Wow!" Rebekah said. "Let's go to the lake and check

them out!"

"No way!" Sophie said. "I don't want to follow those dumb boys! Let's go see the horses. We can sign up for our rides." She pointed to the map. "Here's the stable."

"I vote for the horses, too. Race you," I said.

I got there first and almost bumped into a girl who was walking out of the stable, holding her nose.

"Pheeew! That place stinks!" she yelled, rushing by me.

We stepped inside. A musty, sweaty smell hung in the air. Horses stood in stalls, munching on hay. Beyond the stalls was a large open circular area.

"This looks just like the stables on TV!" Sophie said.

"Check out those pitchforks, ropes, and saddles." Rebekah motioned to the walls.

But I only had eyes for the horses. They were beautiful. "I want to ride that reddish brown one," I said, pointing to the closer one. "But the shiny black ones are awesome too."

"I want to ride that black one," Sophie cried. "He's terrific."

Two counselors were brushing horses in the center of the stable. The horses' long beautiful manes gleamed. One of the counselors looked up and smiled at us.

"Welcome to FSC. I'm Kayla and this is Josh. Do you want to sign up to ride tomorrow?"

"Yes!" We called out together.

She pulled out a clipboard and we told her our names.

"Great! Now we'll show you around the stable, give you some riding and safety tips, and take you outside for a short lesson. That way you'll be ready for a fun time tomorrow."

"How many horses do you have?" Sophie asked after we finished the tour.

"We have twenty-five horses, all different colors and sizes," Josh replied. "They're gentle and love kids."

"Terrific!" Sophie yelled. Rebekah and I giggled.

Instantly one of the horses snorted, pawed the floor, and nervously tossed his head. The other horse flattened his ears back and rolled his eyes.

"Easy," Kayla said. "Girls, you have to keep your voices down, and try not to make sudden movements around the horses. They get frightened and spook easily."

"Oops," Sophie whispered.

"Come on," Kayla said, "we'll take these three horses. They're ready to go." Looking at me, she said, "Since you like Big Red, he's all yours." She was pointing to the chestnut horse.

"Awesome," I said in a low voice.

"You'll need protective riding helmets." Josh handed them to us. "Put these on and buckle the chinstrap up tight."

This was so cool!

"Can we touch the horses?" I asked.

"Yes, but always approach a horse from the front so he can see you," Josh warned.

Sophie, Rebekah, and I gently stroked Big Red's nose.

"Ooooh, it's soft!" Sophie chuckled.

"I know how to ride. I've done it lots of times," Rebekah said.

"It's easy once you get used to it," Kayla said. "By the time you go home, you'll all be pros," she joked. "Now, we'll show you how to mount and dismount."

Josh showed Sophie and me how to hold on to the saddle, place our left foot in the stirrup, and swing our right leg across the horse's back.

"Now you have a go at it."

Sophie had trouble getting her foot in the stirrup. "I can't do it," she cried.

Kayla placed a mounting block on the left side of the horse. "Try this."

"That's more like it! This is a tall horse!" Sophie said.

Kayla placed a block by my horse too.

"Okay, you're ready to ride." Kayla gestured at the other two counselors. "Say hello to Tim and Gabby, your riding instructors. They're going to lead your horses until you're ready to ride on your own. I'll help Rebekah on her horse."

Gabby came over to me. I stepped on the block, placed my left foot into the stirrup, grabbed the saddle, and threw my right leg over it. She adjusted the stirrups and showed me how to hold the reins.

"Wow! This is really high up!" Sophie was the last one lifted up. "I'm a little scared," she said, looking down at Tim.

"Don't worry, we'll walk the horses outside and slowly lead them up the trail so you get a feel for riding," Gabby said.

"Rebekah, do you want to ride ahead of us, since you know how to ride?" Tim asked. "I'll keep an eye on you."

"Yes, I'll go ahead," she answered, beaming.

"It'll only take about ten minutes. Sit up straight, relax, and hold on. Tell us if you want to get off," Tim said.

Sophie and I rode side by side on the trail outside the stable. Rebekah was a few feet ahead of us. She *does* know how to ride. Her long blonde hair hung from under the riding cap.

"This is so much fun," I called to Gabby. She smiled back at me.

When the practice session ended, Tim and Gabby led us back inside the stable. They helped us dismount the way we'd practiced earlier. "All three of you were super," Gabby said.

"I can't wait until tomorrow," Rebekah said. "I'm going to ride fast!"

"This was terrific!" Sophie said. "I'm not scared anymore."

"Report here tomorrow after the morning group session," Kayla said.

When we got back to the cabin, Wendy was standing at the door waiting for us.

"Good. You guys stay here until I get back. I have to run to the main cabin for something," she said. Then left.

Riding was so much fun I had forgotten all about Liz.

When we entered the cabin, there she was, her chubby body sitting humped over on *my* cot.

Sophie smiled and ran over to Liz.

"Hi, my name is—"

"Get away from me!" Liz pulled back, her face twisted. She threw both arms up. "I don't want anything to do with any of you. Leave me alone."

Sophie jumped back. The other girls who had entered the cabin slowly backed away.

"I hope she doesn't say anything to me," one girl murmured.

"I don't want to be her partner," another girl said under her breath.

I stood squarely by my cot and said, "Liz, that's my cot. You need to get over on your own cot."

Without saying a word, she got off my cot and flopped down on hers, turning her back to us.

Wendy opened the door of the cabin. "Okay," she said. "Let's get in a circle on the floor, introduce ourselves, and go over the camp rules."

Liz didn't move.

There was a sharp knock on the door. A voice rang out, "Elizabeth Madison, come with me, please."

Liz stomped past us and bumped the side of her leg into Sophie's back.

"Stop!" Sophie cried out. "You're mean."

Liz turned and smirked back at Sophie, then she slammed the door as hard as she could on the way out.

The whole room sighed.

"I hope she *never* comes back," Rebekah said.

I wished the same thing.

Chapter Ten

After Liz left, things went back to normal. We went over the rules and read the schedule of activities for the rest of the day.

"Just in case you forget," Wendy pointed. "The FSC guidelines are posted on the wall. The red telephone is for emergencies only. When you pick up the receiver, it connects you to the emergency service station. Not the main cabin. Any questions?"

We shook our heads.

"Okay! Let's get acquainted. Everyone say your name and what you plan to do tomorrow. After that, we'll go to the main cabin for our shots and dinner."

Wendy picked up a green beanbag and tossed it from her left hand to her right hand. "I'll throw this to the first girl, and then she'll toss it to whoever she wants when she's done. I'll go last."

She threw the green beanbag to a girl with long, black

wavy hair.

"My name is Maria Garcia. I'm going on my first hayride ever." Up in the air went the bag.

"I'm Ashley Louise Williams." Big round dimples marked both her cheeks. "I'm going hayriding tomorrow with Maria, my new friend." Ashley's brown eyes sparkled.

The bag zoomed through the center of the group and Rebekah caught it.

"This is the first time I've ever stayed away from home. My name is Rebekah Cain. I'm going horseback riding with Portia and Sophie."

Sophie clapped her hands and giggled. "Terrific!" she said, ducking as the bag almost flew by her. "I'm Sophie Chow. I just learned how to give myself shots three weeks ago, I don't like to." She looked down, caught Rebekah's worried look, and smiled at her. "Last year when I turned seven, I went a kazillion miles to China to visit my great-grandfather. It was so fun! I'm going horseback riding tomorrow, too." She pretended to wind up like a baseball pitcher and threw the bag to me.

We chuckled and rolled our eyes.

I caught the bag, but it bounced out of my hands. I hoped no one noticed they were shaking. "My name is Portia Grace Maddox," I said, picking up the beanbag. My voice shook a little too. "I'm going riding with Rebekah and Sophie tomorrow."

My eyes met Wendy's. With relief, I threw the bag to her.

She grinned and caught it. "Great job, campers! You saved the best person for last—me! Just kidding." We laughed. "You already know I'm Wendy Zimmerman. I was diagnosed with diabetes when I was six. You chose the right place. I love FSC. I would come here even if I didn't have a job as your counselor."

"Hey, guys. Let's make a deal," I said to my new buddies, even though I was still a little nervous. "Let's always be friends, love FSC like Wendy does, and when we get old enough, become counselors like her too."

Still in the circle, we leaned in and put our right hands together to seal the pact.

Then we washed our hands and faces and headed to the main cabin. Everything we needed for our diabetic care was laid out on a long table and was labeled with our names.

Wendy pointed to the table. "Get in line, please. Everyone has her own cotton swabs and you know what to do when you're finished. Any questions?"

All of us said "No" except Sophie.

Two members from the FSC medical staff stood beside the table.

"I might need help," Sophie said in a shaky voice. "I just started giving myself shots three weeks ago. Is that okay?"

Nurse White nodded and rubbed the top of Sophie's head. "That's why we're here, to help you."

"Terrific!" Sophie said.

We laughed and acted silly as we passed through the line. I looked around for Liz but didn't see her. Where was she?

After dinner, Wendy took us to the campfire. Lots of boys and girls sat in a circle around a stack of firewood ready to be lit. Our group had just settled down when Liz, led by a counselor, joined us. She sat down next to Wendy without looking at us.

Sophie jumped up, pointing and yelling, "They're lighting the campfire! Look! Look!"

Suddenly, the fire flared—red, orange, and yellow flames— lit up the sky. *Pop! Pop! Pop!*

The smoke blew into my face. I jumped up and turned my head to get away from it. There stood Liz, motionless, staring straight ahead.

Why did she have to be so mean? Why can't she have fun like the rest of us?

Mrs. Jacobs, the camp director, interrupted my thoughts with the welcome speech. The activities started with singing "FSC, You and Me," the camp song.

The drums beat loudly. *Boom! Boom! Boom!*

Twelve counselors dressed in bright red tops, orange waistbands and brown pants made a ring around the fire. We watched as they danced to the beat of the drums.

When the dancing ended, we met in small groups. Everyone told jokes or tall tales and shared their adventures from the day. Everyone except Liz, that is. She sat quietly, hunched over, staring at the ground, poking her finger in the dirt.

"Let's all dance around the campfire!" a counselor shouted.

We jumped up and danced around the fire in a big circle.

Too soon, the bugle played, signaling it was time to go back to our cabins. We had to test our blood sugar, eat a snack, and get ready for bed.

Back in cabin four, in the midst of cleaning up for bed, Maria cried out, "Where's Liz? She's not here. Maybe we should go look—"

The door flew open and in walked Liz. She didn't speak. Eyes glued to the floor, she marched to her chest, pulled out pajamas, and disappeared into the bathroom. We all stared at each other. Soon she came out, flopped down on her cot, and pulled the covers over her head.

"Did you guys have fun today?" Wendy asked.

"Yes. It was a blast," said Ashley. "I can't wait till tomorrow!"

"Shut up!" Liz sat up. "Can't you see I'm trying to sleep? You make me sick. You're all morons." She turned her back to us and covered her head again.

"That's not necessary, Liz," Wendy said. Turning to us, she continued. "I'm glad you guys had a great first day."

Rebekah made a face and hit her forehead with the palm of her hand.

The mood was spoiled. No one spoke as we got into our cots.

I opened my diary.

Dear Diary,

FSC is the bomb! It is the best camp in the whole world. I've met new friends. How cool is that? I enjoyed all the fun things I did today. I can't wait until tomorrow. I'm going horseback riding! Who's Liz's partner? Has she made any friends? Why does she always come in with a counselor? Oh well, I'm not going to let Liz ruin my stay here.

—Sleeping Next to a Troublemaker

I put my diary back in the chest of drawers.

The lights went out.

My brain, exhausted from all the activities of the day, wanted to shut down, but questions continued to whirl in my head.

Where did Liz go when she is not with us? What was she doing? Was she up to something?

Chapter Eleven

The bugle woke us up early the next morning. We made up the cots, put away our things, and washed up.

"Don't forget, Sophie," I reminded her. "You, me, and Rebekah are going horseback riding today."

"How can I forget?" Sophie bounced up and down. "I'm so excited! I couldn't sleep last night."

There was a knock at the door. "Elizabeth Madison, come with me please," someone called from the other side.

Liz left the cabin without a word.

I sighed.

"Where's she going?" Ashley asked under her breath.

"Nurse Fisher will be here in a few minutes to supervise our shots," Wendy told us. "The area where we usually take them in the main cabin is set up for us to watch a video, so the nurse is bringing all our supplies here."

A few minutes later, the nurse walked in.

"Are you ready for your shots?" she asked.

Sophie frowned. "I might need a little help because this time I should get an injection in the upper arm."

"No problem," Nurse Fisher said. "I'll help you."

"Terrific." Sophie's voice trembled.

All of us took our shots, and Wendy did too! Afterwards, we put our used cotton balls and needles in the red plastic container.

"Okay, let's go eat breakfast," Wendy said.

"My favorite!" I said when I saw the menu. "I love breakfast burritos. Egg, bacon, fried potato, and cheese wrapped in a flour tortilla—deeelicious!"

After breakfast, we saw a short video on diabetes. I learned that one of Mom's favorite actresses, Halle Berry, has diabetes, and Nick Jonas, one of the Jonas Brothers, has diabetes too.

When the video ended, a counselor asked, "What's the rule about diabetes we should remember?"

We answered together, "Eating raises your blood glucose level; exercise and insulin lower it."

"Yes! Yes!" all the counselors yelled back.

I sat up, my chest proudly sticking out, because I knew how to take care of myself.

Next, I went with a group of kids to the craft room. I wanted to make some jewelry for Grandma Ruth, Mom, and Sarah. The smell of glue and paint greeted my nose. Kids wearing smocks stood around a long table, giggling, talking, and painting their presents.

"What do you want to make?" the craft counselor asked.

"I need to make a hair bow, bracelet, and three necklaces," I said. "I'm not sure what I want to make for my dad."

"Here, I'll help you cut ceramic pieces using this machine," he said.

After I chose the patterns, we cut them out. Then I used high-gloss paint to put a finish on them. I made a picture frame for Dad. It took an hour for the paint to dry.

When the gifts were finished, I left to meet the girls and to test my blood sugar.

"Hi, Portia," Rebekah called. "Where were you?"

"In the craft room making presents for my family and necklaces for me. They are beautiful."

After we tested our blood sugar, we went to get our snacks. "Yesterday I had string cheese, a banana, crackers, and milk." Sophie shrugged. "I hope they have something different today."

"The midmorning snack today is beef jerky, crackers and cheese, and grapes," I reported, reading the menu.

"Yummy!" Sophie said.

After eating, we headed to the stable for our horseback rides.

"This isn't the same horse I rode yesterday. This horse is too big for me to ride." Sophie whispered to me, "I'm afraid to ride by myself. I didn't get enough practice yesterday."

"Let Kayla know," I suggested, "and maybe she'll bring you a different one."

Sophie, never shy for words, said to Kayla, "This horse is too big. I need the one I rode yesterday."

Kayla saddled up the horse Sophie wanted and gave her a leg up.

"Thank you," Sophie said with a nervous grin.

Rebekah and I rode slowly behind Sophie, and Tim and Gabby rode behind us.

I rode the chestnut horse again. He was gorgeous! I tried to hold the reins steady with my trembling hands.

"This is way high up!" I called to Rebekah.

"It is, but don't look down," Rebekah replied. "You'll be fine. Chill out, keep your eyes up and enjoy the ride."

We rode slowly up and down the trails. *Clippity-clop! Clippity-clop!* echoed the horses' hooves. The wind brushed across my face.

This was so awesome!

When the hour was up, we headed back to the stable. My bottom was sore.

Six kids stood outside the stable listening to riding instructions. It was their turn to ride. Tim and Gabby walked our horses around the stable, cooling them off before they groomed them, and put them back in their stalls.

We skipped to the main cabin. It was time to test our blood sugar again.

"I'm hungry," Sophie yelled. "Let's run!"

While we were eating, Liz came to sit at the table. She took a seat far away from us and stared down in her plate as she ate.

"I had fun today!" Maria grinned. "We went on a hayride and saw everything. The ride took us all around FSC."

"What did you do this morning, Liz?" Sophie called.

Liz rolled her eyes at Sophie. "Forget you! Don't talk to me."

"Me, Rebekah, and Sophie went horseback riding!" I told her.

Liz flashed a look at me. Our eyes met. Did she want to ride with us? Should I ask her? Would the girls want her to go?

After we ate, we walked around, checking out things for us to do. When we got back to our cabin, a counselor was waiting at the door.

She let us in, and we heard someone sobbing. We looked around but didn't see anyone.

"Elizabeth Madison, are you ready?" the counselor called into the cabin. "Time to go."

Liz walked out of the bathroom. Her green eyes were puffy.

"What's wrong? Why are you crying?" Sophie asked.

Liz walked right up close to Sophie, bent over so they would be face to face and said, "Mind your own business. If you don't leave me alone, I'm gonna beat you up." She stuck out her tongue at us, turned, and stomped out the door.

"She's sooo mean," Sophie said. "Do you think she has any friends?"

"I don't think she's having a good time," I answered. "I feel sorry for her."

"You do?" Sophie asked.

I didn't answer. I turned and walked quickly out of the cabin. I wanted to forget Liz's anger. Sophie jogged behind me.

Chapter Twelve

My gaze roamed around the cafeteria—good, no Liz. We took our shots.

"Are you hungry?" Sophie asked.

"I'm so hungry I could eat a horse!" We both burst out laughing.

We went to table four and joined the girls for dinner. Neither one of us said anything about Liz.

The day ended too soon. After dinner, we huddled around the campfire. A counselor escorted Liz to the group. We sang the FSC song and danced around the fire, then walked back to our cabin, without Liz, and got ready for bed.

About twenty minutes before the nine-thirty "lights-out," the door opened and in Liz walked.

"Good night, Elizabeth," the counselor said and closed the door.

Without a look, Liz went to her chest, pulled out her pajamas and hairbrush, and went to the shower. A few minutes later, she came out and got into her cot. Her eyes were red again. What's wrong with her?

The lights went out. I was so tired. I went right to sleep.

The next morning, the bugle startled me awake. Liz had already gone.

Rebekah, Sophie, and I went to the game room and played video games. Then we went swimming and later saw a puppet show.

We made plans to go horseback riding. I remembered Liz's flash of interest.

"Come and walk with me to the cabin," I said to Sophie and Rebekah. "I want to do something." I thought. Liz might be in the cabin.

"We'll wait for you by the flagpole," said Rebekah. "We can see you."

"Okay. I'll be back." I headed for our cabin.

When I opened the door, I heard quiet sobbing. Wendy was sitting on Liz's cot with her arm around her shoulder.

"Why are you crying?" I asked Liz.

"Liz is having a hard time," Wendy said.

"What's wrong?" I sat down beside Liz.

"I want to go horseback riding and I'm not allowed to." Liz's voice shook. "'Cause I don't have any hiking boots. I can only go to the areas where there are no pebbles or small rocks.

It's no fun being cooped up like a baby."

I felt bad for her. "Didn't you read the list of clothing that you were supposed to bring to camp? Why didn't you bring boots?"

"Yeah, I read the list." Liz wiped away tears. "I thought if I didn't bring them, Mom would take me back home. I didn't want to come to this old camp. She said I wasn't going back home, and I had to stay in the areas where I didn't have to wear hard shoes. That's no fun."

"I have a pair of hiking boots that I'll let you borrow."

"Portia, that's so nice of you," Wendy said.

"Why?" Liz shot a long hard look at me. "Why would you do that? You don't even like me. The other girls hate me too."

I shrugged. "I know you want to have a good time, and I don't want to be mean to you." I walked over to my chest and pulled out the hiking boots.

"Come here and try them on. They have shoestrings, so if they're too big, we can tie them tight, but if they're too small, I can't help you."

Liz hesitated.

"Go on. Give it a try," Wendy urged. "Can't hurt."

Liz slowly walked over, took off her right sneaker, picked up a boot, and slid her foot into it.

A gigantic grin came over her face. "It fits! It fits!" she shouted at the top of her lungs. She quickly put on the left boot.

I noticed space in the back of her heels. "Liz, let's put some tissue in front of your toes and tie the shoestrings tight. Then they will fit better."

To my surprise, Liz jumped up and hugged me. She has such small feet for a big girl.

She ran to the bathroom and brought the whole roll of toilet tissue back. Wendy and I packed the toes with tissue.

"There," Wendy said. "Tie up the strings."

"Do you think the girls will let me go riding with them?" Liz asked as she tied the strings.

"Yes, I think so. Let's hurry. They're waiting for me by the flagpole."

I grabbed Liz's hand and ran for the door. Wendy followed.

"Is it okay for Liz to come ride with us?" I asked the girls. "She has on the right shoes."

Rebekah stared at Liz.

"It's okay with me if you and Rebekah want her to come with us," Sophie blurted out.

We all looked at Rebekah. "Okay by me," She finally said and shrugged.

"I'm glad you girls worked that out," said Wendy. She waved goodbye. The four of us headed to the stable.

This was one of my best days at camp. I almost forgot how much my butt hurt from the horseback ride the day before. My new friends are great! Even Liz smiled a few times!

That night at the campfire, when Liz joined our group, she sat next to me. She stared straight ahead. "I … I want to thank you for letting me wear your boots."

"You're welcome. Where do you go when you're not with us?"

Liz stared down at the ground. "I have to go to the nurse so she can take my blood sugar and give me my shots. When Mom told me I had to learn to give myself shots, I was so scared. I couldn't do it. I screamed and cried so much that she stopped asking me."

"When Mom and Dad told me that I had to learn, I was scared, too," I shared.

"Maybe when we get back home, I could come over to your house and help you like my cousin, Sarah, helped me."

Liz faced me. "Would you do that? Would you ask your mom if you could come over for a visit? I've been watching how the nurses give me my shots. I learned a lot already."

"Yes, when I come back from visiting my grandma, I'll call you and see when I can come over. I know we'll have fun."

That night Liz and I became friends. We exchanged phone numbers.

The next two days, Liz went with Sophie, Rebekah, and me swimming, horseback riding, and hiking.

She even came to our small group and started to talk to us.

"When Portia comes home from visiting her grandma, she is going to visit me," she announced.

Liz smiled more and talked to Sophie, who was a little chatterbox and could bring a smile to anyone's face.

The last night of camp, I wrote,

Dear Diary,

I'm sad this super week is over. My new friends promised to keep in touch and come back next summer. Even Liz said she wanted to come back! Will she stop bullying kids at school? I hope she has changed. I had so much fun. I like riding the horses the most.

Sarah would be proud of me. Is she still following her routine?

I miss Mom and Dad. The last time I saw them, they were sad and not speaking to each other. Are things better?

—Happy Camper Anxious to Go Home

While we were waiting for our parents to pick us up, Rebekah and Sophie the Terrific came over to say goodbye. We hugged each other and promised to call.

A few minutes later, Liz came and stood next to me.

"Thank you for letting me wear your hiking boots and being nice to me. I hope you can come over for a visit," she said.

"You're welcome. I knew you wanted to have fun, and we all had a good time. When I get back from my grandma's house, I'll call you."

Liz handed me a package tied with a pink bow. "I made a bracelet for you in the craft room yesterday. Please take it. I had B.F.F. engraved on it."

"You didn't have to do that!"

"I wanted to. I know I've been mean to you and the other girls. I told them I was sorry for acting so mean. Now I feel much better. I'm going to learn to give myself insulin, too."

Liz's mom pulled up. They put her bags in the car.

Waving goodbye, Liz said, "Best Friends Forever!"

I grinned. "Forever."

Liz's mom smiled and said, "Thank you," then drove off.

I couldn't wait to see my parents. I had a lot to tell them, especially how I slept next to a bully and survived.

I had a great time at camp, but I missed my parents, and I

missed sleeping in my own bed.

Were Mom and Dad getting along? Would things be better between them when I got home?

Chapter Thirteen

When Mom arrived, I gave her a big hug. "Where's Daddy? Why didn't he come with you?"

"Your dad had to work." Mom's voice was soft as usual and very low. Her eyes tired and far away and she looked thinner.

Things had gotten worse.

On the drive home, I told her about my week, hoping to make her smile. But I couldn't. She just answered, "Oh, really," "is that so," and "you don't say," to everything. I could tell something was on her mind, but I was so happy and wanted to tell her about camp. I talked all the way home. I didn't realize that we had driven home so quickly until we pulled into the driveway. It seemed like it had taken forever to get to camp and that coming home took half the time.

Dad's car was in the driveway.

"Daddy's home!" I yelled.

The front door opened, and Dad stepped out. He walked to my side of the car and opened the door. His arms reached for me, and we hugged.

"Did you have a good time, Baby Girl? You'll have to tell me all about camp."

The words Dad spoke were happy, but I heard the same pain in his voice that was in Mom's.

"What's the matter, Daddy?"

"Nothing, I'm glad you're home."

That night, it was hard getting to sleep. My parents' sad faces kept coming into my head.

The next morning I slept in because I hadn't fallen asleep until way past midnight. When I went to the kitchen, Dad and Mom were sitting at the kitchen table not looking at each other. Had something happened while I was away? Maybe my presents would make them happy.

"Mom, I made you this bracelet." I held it up and turned it over in my hand. "Daddy, I made this picture frame and put my picture in it for you."

"Thank you, Baby Girl. I love it." Dad kissed me. "I'm going to put it on my nightstand."

"Portia, I'll always treasure this bracelet." Mom placed it on her arm and modeled it. "What did you make for yourself?"

I smiled. "I made two necklaces for me and one for Grandma."

"I know how much you love jewelry," Mom added. "Thank

you for my bracelet. Now, tell us more about camp."

While eating breakfast, I told my parents about how much fun I'd had, about Rebekah, Sophie the Terrific and Liz. "You would be proud of me. I rode Big Red, a beautiful chestnut horse, all up and down the trails."

"You are growing into quite a young lady," Dad said.

Later that morning, I washed clothes and cleaned my room. On Sunday, Mom and I were flying to Port Saint Charles to spend a week with Grandma Ruth.

"Mom, can we go to Sarah's house so I can give her the hair bow I made for her?"

"Yes, as soon as you're ready."

When Mom and I were on the way to Sarah's, I asked, "Are you ready to go visit Grandma?"

"Yes, I need to get away to think and rest."

"Did you love being a kid back there?"

"I had the best dad and mom in the world. My dad loved all the kids in the neighborhood. He built the tree house in the backyard you like to play in with your friends and cousins." A big grin came over Mom's face. "He put a swing up for us. Kids were always at my house, and I had lots of friends to play with when I was growing up."

We pulled into Sarah's driveway and Mom was still smiling. It felt good seeing a smile on her face.

Mom and I could only stay two hours with Sarah and her parents. We had to get back home and finish packing. But Sarah and I had enough time to laugh and share our latest adventures.

Early Sunday morning, Dad took us to the airport.

"Portia, tell Grandma Ruth and the family I said hello," Dad said.

"I will, Daddy."

Dad kissed me goodbye, but not Mom. They always kiss when they leave each other.

"Mom, can I sit next to the window?" I asked after we boarded the airplane.

"Yes, I know you're going to sleep. You always do when we fly," she answered.

I smiled and nodded.

Grandma's house looked just like it did on our last visit. Green shutters held the four front windows snugly to the white house, and the short shrubs pressed tightly against it. The velvet grass in the front yard was neatly cut. A giant tree that stood in the backyard hovered over the house. Grandma's red rose bushes bloomed in the yard. Her house was much older than ours.

Grandma stood on the porch when Mom pulled the rental car into the driveway.

"My, you two ladies are a beautiful sight for my eyes!" Her face lit up and she laughed. "Portia, you have your dad's hazel eyes and your mom's curly brown hair. The older you get the more you look like them!"

We gave her a kiss and carried our bags inside.

"Something smells good," Mom said.

"I made toasted peanut butter sandwiches."

"Yummy!" I said. "Lucky it's time for my snack." The smell of the sandwiches made my mouth water.

Mom and I put our suitcases in the bedrooms and hurried to the kitchen, where Grandma waited with our milk and sandwiches.

"Grandma, look, I made this necklace at camp for you." I held it up for her to see. She sat still while I fastened it around her neck.

"This is just what I need. Thank you so much, Portia. I can wear it with my purple dress."

I told Grandma about camp and Liz, the bully from school.

"Baby, I knew you'd be fine at camp and you were!" She grinned and hugged me. "I'm so proud of you."

The next morning after eating breakfast, Grandma asked, "Grace, are you and Portia ready to go see a few of your cousins?"

"Yes, we are," Mom replied.

"I'm ready," I said. "Haven't seen some of them in a long time. Think they'll remember me?"

"Yes, I told them you were coming to stay a week," Grandma said. "You're going to have fun."

The days were busy with lots of visits. We called on relatives, and they came to see us at Grandma's house. One morning we visited the port and watched the huge ships come in and unload their cargo.

Even though I enjoyed seeing my family, this trip to Grandma's was sort of strange. A lot of times, Grandma and Mom would be talking quietly, and when I came into the room, they'd stop. This had never happened on other visits.

I heard these hush-hush talks late in the nights, too. On the last night of our visit, Grandma and Mom talked in the kitchen again. Their low voices crept down the hall, through my bedroom walls, and into my ears.

"Did you and Russell talk to Portia about this? You know you should tell her," Grandma said.

"No, I just learned about it, and it hurts so bad. I'm not ready to tell her yet. How can I explain it to her when I don't understand it myself?"

What were they talking about? I wondered if this had anything to do with the time I overheard Dad on the phone saying, "I love you too, Baby Girl." When I'd asked him about it he gave me a hug and told me to go to bed. I never asked any more questions, but I still know he was hiding something.

On the last day of our visit, we had a cookout in Grandma's backyard. Uncle Luke did the cooking. Everyone said he was the best cook in the county. He had blue ribbons all over his house from the county fairs to prove it.

"Eat up!" he called out, putting the hamburgers, hot dogs, and ribs on the table, and we did.

Uncle Luke is Grandma's only brother. They have a sister named Myra. All of them have salt-and-pepper hair. Grandma Ruth and Aunt Myra wear glasses. Grandma looked like a dwarf next to Uncle Luke, even with her black pumps on. Since Uncle Luke's wife had died last year, he and Grandma had grown closer than before—if that was possible.

When the cookout ended, it was sad saying goodbye to all my relatives. Mom acted as if she didn't want to leave. I didn't want to leave Grandma, but school would be starting in two weeks, and I was ready to go home.

We didn't talk while we packed our suitcases. Somehow leaving Grandma and Uncle Luke seemed harder this time.

The next morning we put our bags in the car. Grandma Ruth said, "Tell Russell hello and I hope to see him soon."

"I will, Grandma," I said. "I love you."

Grandma's hug was a little tighter and longer than usual.

Dad picked us up at the airport, and he and Mom didn't say anything to each other on the drive home.

This made me feel more than sad. This time I was a little angry. I knew something was wrong, but they wouldn't tell me what it was.

A sick feeling crawled into my stomach. I pushed it aside, hoping that it would disappear by the time we got home. Little did I know this feeling marked the beginning of an even bigger crisis in my life.

Chapter Fourteen

Another sign came the next day when I asked about shopping. "Can we *please* go shopping for my school clothes and supplies?" I begged. "It's only two weeks before school starts."

"Yes, it's that time again," Mom answered absentmindedly.

She had been different last year. She'd insisted that we shop early, and she'd even helped me match all my outfits. We'd laughed and joked about which ones went together and which ones looked silly. She had even bought a dress for herself.

But the way things had been going lately, I wasn't sure what to expect this time. It seemed like shopping for my school clothes was the last thing on her mind.

This afternoon, we didn't laugh or chitchat like before. She picked up a blouse, held it up to her body, and put it back.

"How do you like this dress?" I held up a purple and orange dress with smiling faces all over it.

"Whatever you think, dear." Mom sighed. "It's your choice."

She wasn't paying attention. She *never* liked smiling faces on clothes. She always said, "Only a crazy person would wear a smiling face on their clothes, Portia. The person should smile—not their clothes."

"Mom, when we were at Grandma's house, what were you talking about late at night?"

Mom's eyebrows flew up and she stared into my eyes. "I just needed someone to talk to. You know that Mom and I confide in each other."

"Can't you tell me?" I pushed.

"I needed to discuss this problem with Mom. When you get older, you and I will talk about everything like Mom and I do, but right now this problem isn't one I feel comfortable discussing with you." She rubbed my chin. "Let's get back to these clothes or we'll never get out of this mall."

"Why don't you and Dad smile and laugh together like you used to?" I tried one more time to get her to tell me.

"Your dad has been busy at work. He's tired when he comes home." She looked away from me. Her voice trembled. "We're trying to work things out. It's complicated but getting a little better."

I didn't believe her. Mom said the right words, but her eyes held a secret.

Summer ended, school started, and I got busy. My diabetes

was under control. The swim team continued in middle school, and I made new friends. I forgot about that conversation for a little while.

As the weather turned cold and night came too quickly, the unhappy look stayed on Mom's face. She didn't smile or laugh, and Dad was hardly ever home.

The next sign came one night when I got out of bed to get water. I overheard Mom and Dad talking.

"Is that what you think?" Dad's voice rose. "You know I love you and Portia more than anything."

"Russell, you should have told me." Mom's soft voice cracked. "Why didn't you?"

It sounded like she was crying. I wanted to run to the kitchen and yell at both of them. "What's wrong with you two? Why are you mad at each other? Why can't you two be nice to each other?"

I got back in bed and put my head under the covers, trying to blot out their words. No way could I sleep now. I tossed and turned for hours. I went over the last few months in my mind, and now a lot of things made sense. Mom and Dad really were mad at each other.

I stayed busy with school and my friends, trying to escape the sadness and anger in my house. We never went anywhere together anymore, not even to Sarah's house.

For a while, I tried to avoid the problems at home, and then one Saturday morning, when I went to the kitchen, Mom and Dad sat at the table with frowns on their faces.

Finally, it happened! Dad waved his hand to a chair. "Come and sit down, Baby Girl."

I took a seat as far away from them as I could and swallowed. Their frowns deepened. *What now?*

"Your dad and I have something to tell you." Mom looked at me and spoke in a quiet voice. "It's time to let you know what's happened. There's no easy way to say it."

My mind ran ahead. What were they going to tell me? Did this have something to do with those quiet talks at Grandma's? Or when Dad called someone "Baby Girl" on the phone? Or how—I couldn't hear what Mom was saying. I saw her mouth moving.

"… and we decided that a separation would be the best thing for right now. It'll give us time to sort things—"

"What?" I cut in. "Are you and Dad getting a divorce?" A chill ran through my body.

"No, Baby Girl," Dad quickly replied. "We are not talking about divorce."

"Yes, you are!" I cried. "Mary Ann's mother and father separated, and Mr. Walton married someone else. She says she doesn't like her stepmom, and she never goes to visit her dad. What's wrong? Don't you two love me anymore? Is this my fault?"

Mom stood up, moved near me, and put her hand on mine. "No, Portia, it's not about you. You haven't done anything to cause this problem. This is something your dad and I have to figure out. Please give us time to work through this."

Dad came and stood by me and put his arm around my shoulder. "Portia, I love you, and I'll always be your father. That'll never change. Something happened a long time ago before you were born, and your mom and I are having problems with it. We need to come to terms with it." He looked down and took my hand. "We can't keep going on like we've been trying to do the past couple of months. It isn't good for any of us like this." He squeezed my hand.

Mom took my right hand, and Dad held my left. Both held on tight.

I jerked my hands away, ran to my room, and closed the door. I crawled in bed and cried until my head ached.

Later, I went to the kitchen for a snack.

Mom was washing dishes. "Portia, I know this is upsetting news." She wiped her hands and hugged me. "We'll work this out. We're going to get through this and please don't forget to take care of yourself. You need to be strong."

I tried to say something, but no words would come out of

my mouth. I nearly choked on my sandwich.

After finishing my juice, I hurried back to my room.

I took the photo album off my desk, and slowly turned the pages, looking for answers. There was a photo of me on my first bike, with Dad holding me. He had helped me learn to ride it.

Warm tears ran down my face. I wiped them away and turned the page. Here we were again. I had on my new pink skates. Dad had pushed me until I learned to skate by myself.

The weekend came when Dad moved out. After he packed his things, he came into my room. "Portia, I know you're sad. Your mom and I are too. We're trying to work this problem out. If we're apart, we might be able to think more clearly and won't keep hurting each other. I'll visit next week. You have my number. I'll call you every night. You can call me whenever you want."

I just sat there. I felt numb. Dad went into the garage. I heard the car start.

I walked to my window and watched him back out of the driveway. He headed down the street away from me. His car slowly became a small blur in the distance.

Tears rolled down my cheeks. I was alone.

Dear Diary,

Dad's gone. It hurts so bad. I love my father. How could he want to leave me? Did he stop loving me? Doesn't he want to be my dad anymore? What am I going to do without him? What can I do to make him come back to me? I can't believe we're not a family anymore. What am I going to do?

—So Sad

Mom came into my room and put her arms around me. "I know this isn't easy for you. You love your dad so much, and he loves you. We both do."

The next few months, I tried to do things to get my parents back together. When Dad came over to see me, I showed him the good grades that I'd earned in school. I asked, "When are you coming back home?"

He said, "I hope soon, Baby Girl." But he didn't come back.

I begged Grandma to help when she called me. She said it was between Mom and Dad.

When we had our school fundraiser for the local diabetes association, my class won a pizza party because we raised the most money. I had worked hard to help plan a walk-a-thon, and I'd received more donations than anyone in my class.

That weekend I asked Mom, "When is Dad coming back to live with us?"

"I don't know, dear," she answered. "We're still trying to work things out."

Nothing I tried worked. I was beginning to feel like we would never get back together. By the last month of school, I was a walking zombie. I got up, went to school, came home, did my homework, ate dinner, and went to bed. My only joys were the calls from Grandma Ruth and my swimming.

Mom tried to cheer me up, but she wasn't happy either. I found myself missing some of my snacks during the day, and once I forgot to take my insulin shot.

Then one day I left my fanny pack with my diabetes kit in it at home. I had to call Mom.

"Would you please bring my pack to school for me? It's on top of my bed."

"Are you all right?

"Yes. I'm sorry. I just forgot it."

"I'll bring it, but please don't ever do that again!" Mom's voice choked. "I have enough to deal with."

For the next few weeks, Mom asked if I were all right. "Are you testing and taking your shots? You know you can't miss any."

"I'm fine. I won't forget my kit anymore," I promised.

Mom pleaded with me to come to talk with her at the kitchen table or to stay after we'd finished eating. I couldn't talk to her about how I felt. I needed to get to Grandma.

The house was empty, without life. Without Dad. What could I do to get my family back together?

Chapter Fifteen

Finally, summer came. I was glad school was out so I could go visit my Grandma.

She was the only one who could calm this storm that had split Mom, Dad, and me up. She'd always been there for me when bad things happened.

When I was seven years old, Champ, my puppy, ran into the street and was killed by a car.

The evening after it happened, Mom put her arms around me. "Portia, we don't understand why things that make us feel sad happen, but they do."

Her words didn't make me feel better.

Dad tried to cheer me up. He didn't help either.

When Grandma Ruth came for a visit two days later, I told her, "Grandma, Champ died two days ago. I miss him so much." She put her hand under my chin and turned my face so I could look into her eyes. "We're going to go in the backyard where your dad set up a memorial to Champ and say a proper goodbye. I want you to come up with the words you want to say to him."

"But I don't know what to say. I'm sad. I miss him."

"When you go to bed tonight, you'll think of the right words."

That night I pulled out my diary and closed my eyes. There was Champ, with his shining, fluffy, golden-brown fur, jumping up and down, wagging his tail. I wrote what I wanted to say to him. I closed the diary and tried to sleep.

Early the next morning, Grandma walked into my room. "Did you write what you're going to say?"

"Yes, Grandma. It's in my diary."

We went outside to Champ's memorial. I opened the diary and read:

Dear Champ,

I miss you. I loved to play with you when I came home from school. You were my friend. I'm sorry I opened the door and you ran into the street. You died because I wasn't able to keep you inside the house.

—Miss you

"May I say a few words?" Grandma asked.

Afraid more tears would come if I spoke, I nodded.

"Champ, we know you're in a better place. We can feel your happy spirit. I miss you, too."

Grandma knelt down, wiped my tears, and gave me a hug. "You know how feisty puppies are. It's their nature to always run and play. Even though sometimes we're tired or sick and don't want to play, they still want to play."

I looked at Grandma. "Yeah, when I was sick, Champ jumped on me all the time wanting to play. He paced up and down the floor wanting me to run and chase after him."

I hugged her back. "Grandma, I'm so glad you're here."

Now I needed her help again with a bigger problem, and I was so glad we were on our way to see her.

"Are you ready to go see Grandma? I am."

"Yes, I'm ready for a visit, too," Mom said. "These past few months have been hard on all three of us." I saw the sad lines around Mom's eyes as she tried to close the suitcase.

"Portia, did you test your sugar?" Mom asked.

"Yes, I'm taking care of myself," I quickly answered her. I didn't want her to worry about me. I didn't forget any more shots.

Sunday evening Dad came over to take us to the airport.

Before we boarded the plane, Dad gave me a hug and whispered, "Baby Girl, we are working on our problem. I love you and always will. Tell Grandma Ruth hello for me. I'll be waiting for you and your mom to come home."

I grabbed Dad around the neck. "I love you too, Daddy. I'll tell Grandma what you said."

"Thank you for bringing us to the airport, Russell," Mom said.

This trip to Grandma's was different from any I'd taken before. I was on a mission to get Dad back home with me no matter what, and the person at the end of this plane ride could help me.

The plane zoomed way up and flew over the fluffy white clouds. After about an hour, the pilot came on the intercom. "Folks, looks like we might have a few bumps ahead. There is reported turbulence about one hundred miles out. Make sure you keep those seatbelts fastened until the seatbelt light goes off."

The airplane shook. A bolt of lightning flashed by my window. The rain beat down on the plane. Butterflies fluttered in my stomach.

This storm was just as upsetting as the one in my life.

Finally, bumps and all, we landed safely. A taxi drove us to Grandma's house.

The wind blew hard. The trees swayed back and forth. Heavy, grayish black clouds lined the sky. I had never seen clouds so dark.

Grandma's house soon came into view. Even though the dark clouds hung over the house, the warm, glowing yellow lights from the windows welcomed me.

Mom and I rushed to the front door. Grandma stood there with a wide grin on her face. The taxi driver brought our bags to the porch, and Mom paid him.

"You girls come in and let me take a look at you," Grandma said, wiping the rain from her glasses.

"Hello, Mom. It's good seeing you."

"My goodness, you two look great!" Grandma hugged Mom first and then me. I wanted her to hold me until the pain went away.

Mom and I carried the suitcases to our rooms while Grandma warmed milk and got snacks ready.

We went into the kitchen and sat at the table. Grandma took a long sip from her cup and looked at me. Did she know how to get Dad back home? I wanted to ask, but I didn't want to be the first to start *that* conversation.

"I heard someone has grown up and is making good grades in school this year," she said.

That was my cue to start talking, but I wanted to talk about Mom and Dad and have her help them fix this problem. I didn't want to talk about me.

I shrugged and mumbled, "It's no big deal."

Grandma sipped her warm milk in silence.

"Daddy came by and took me to the movies last Saturday," I blurted out.

"He did? Your dad is a special man," Grandma said and patted my hand.

Mom put her mug down. "It's been a long day. Let's go to bed and talk tomorrow. Mom, do you need any help?"

"No, you two get some rest."

I went to my room and Mom went to hers. Grandma stayed behind washing the dishes. It hurt not talking to her because I knew she had been waiting all day for her "girls."

As I lay in bed, I heard Grandma humming. Should I go talk to her about my dad? Then the humming stopped.

The house stood still as the wind howled outside and the rain pounded on the roof.

I heard footsteps. The door opened, and Grandma quietly entered my bedroom. She sat on the side of the bed. "Portia, I know all about your mom and dad, and I know it hurts," she said with a soft voice like Mom's. "They're working hard to come to an understanding, and they're going through a lot. I know they still love each other, and God knows they love you. So don't ever think that you're not loved."

I sat up against my pillow. "Why did Dad and Mom have to separate?"

"Well, sometimes we need to be alone to do our best thinking. We need space to sort out our feelings. That's what your mom and dad need now. Let them have their space." Grandma took my hands in hers. "You're growing up, and in time, you'll have to make some important decisions that'll require some deep soul searching, too. Do you remember when you had to decide to take responsibility for giving yourself shots?"

I nodded, and she continued. "Well, you made that decision yourself. Nobody could make you do it." She shifted her body. "I pray that those two stay together, but if they don't, it won't be your fault. It'll be something they just can't work out. I need you to be a little patient and give them time."

"Grandma, it hurts when Mom and Dad don't talk to each other, but I'll try to understand. I want my daddy to come back home. I love you."

Grandma gave me a kiss on the cheek and left the room. I got up and looked out the window. The sky was moonless, starless, almost black. Rain poured down.

I wanted to sleep with Mom or Grandma, but I remembered what Grandma had said about me acting grown up. Fearing she might think I was a baby, I got back in bed, closed my eyes, and listened to the rain beating on the roof.

Grandma's words played over and over in my head. "Give

them time to work things out. They still love each other. They just need time."

I pulled out my diary.

Dear Diary,

It feels good at Grandma's house. Mom and Dad not being together still hurts, but tonight I'm not crying myself to sleep. What can I do to get them back together? Mom's face is always sad, and when Dad comes by to see me, he seems unhappy. Grandma said to give them time. I want to try to do what she asked.

—Trying to be Patient

I closed the diary, placed it under my pillow, and forced myself to relax.

When I woke up the next morning, the wind was still blowing hard. The rain had stopped, but the sky was dark and packed with clouds full of water, ready to burst.

The smell of pancakes drifted down the hall from the kitchen.

"Yummy," I blurted out.

"Are you up, Sleepy Head?" Mom called.

"Yes, I'm getting in the shower," I called back. "I'll be out for breakfast in a sec."

When I got to the kitchen, Mom told me, "The weatherman said there might be a hurricane on the way."

"I hope it passes by us or doesn't do any damage," said Grandma, shaking her head. "I remember the last one. It seemed as if it would never stop raining. The streets flooded, roofs flew off houses, and cars filled with water. But the levee withstood the water, and we didn't lose any lives. I'm sorry you and Portia are here at such a bad time."

"I'm not sorry we're here," I said. "This is where I want to be."

Grandma winked at me. "Who wants some of my potato pancakes?"

Grandma makes the best potato pancakes in the whole wide world.

"I smelled them from the shower, and I'm starving! Grandma, put two on my plate, please?"

"That's my girl!" She hummed as she flipped the pancakes.

Mom smiled, and for a moment, her face changed back to the way I remembered before our trouble started.

I *had* to give Mom and Dad time to fix their problem.

The potato pancakes were light, crisp, and golden brown just the way I liked them. Grandma's homemade maple syrup— delicious.

The lights in the kitchen blinked off and on. The wind howled and shook the house. Thunder roared, and lightning flashed. Mom reached for her cup of coffee and knocked it over. Grandma jumped up, got a wet towel, and cleaned up the mess. "It's really setting bad out there. I hope the storm doesn't get any stronger." Grandma said.

I gulped, scared that Mom and Grandma were scared too. Grandma switched on the TV.

Chapter Sixteen

"Folks, that tropical storm out in the gulf has just been classified as a hurricane. They named it Hurricane Kelly and I'm afraid it's headed for Port Saint Charles. Winds are expected to reach one hundred and twenty miles per hour by the time it touches our shore." The weatherman waved his arms over a map showing arrows twirling in a circle on the TV screen. "We're on hurricane watch. We'll probably have to evacuate."

"That means we have about twenty-four hours or so," Grandma said.

"Will we have to go to Aunt Myra's?" Mom asked.

"If it keeps raining like it is, and this wind gets any stronger, we'll need to leave. With the rain and wind, we get heavy waves in the gulf. The only way we'll be safe is if Hurricane Kelly changes course, and I think it's too late for that."

Grandma and Mom looked worried, and my heart raced. "Grandma, do hurricanes blow houses away?"

"I hope and pray that doesn't happen," she said, rubbing my hand.

"Breaking news!" the weatherman said. "The National Weather Center warned us that this is a big one, folks! Warm air is coming in off the gulf as high pressure builds up and pushes inland."

"What's he talking about, Grandma?"

"Shhh!" Grandma put her finger to her lips. "Let's listen to what he has to say."

The weatherman shuffled some papers. "Hurricane Kelly has just been classified as a category three hurricane. We don't know how much our levee can withstand. We're waiting for word from city officials on when we have to evacuate."

The weatherman adjusted his earpiece. "More breaking news! City officials are telling everyone to start packing for mandatory evacuation. The hurricane is forecasted to reach us in the next thirty-six hours." He leaned into the microphone. "Severe winds are blowing in from the southeast. They're pushing closer and closer to Port Saint Charles."

I shuddered. "Grandma?"

"Grace, call Luke to come and take us to Greensburg. It's time for us to leave."

Mom ran to the phone. "Uncle Luke, this is Grace. Momma wants you to come and take us to Aunt Myra's. Okay, we'll be ready." She hung up the phone. "Let's pack our suitcases. Uncle Luke will be here in an hour, and he wants us to be ready."

My heart pounded as I rushed to pack.

"Momma," Mom called. "Do you need any help?"

"No, I'm just about finished. Call Russell and let him know we're going to Myra's house."

"Okay. Don't forget your medicine," Mom called back.

"I have it in my bags."

Mom went to the phone to call Dad. I wanted to hear but couldn't. I watched. She ran her hand across her forehead two or three times.

"How's Daddy? What did he say?" I asked after she got off the phone.

"He's all right. But he's worried because we're here in this hurricane. He said to tell you he misses you and loves you."

I wished he were with us.

Sitting on top of my suitcase, I turned to Mom. The wind howled and the house shook. "Where's Uncle Luke? How long did he say it'd be before he got here?"

Mom checked our luggage. "He should be here any minute. We'll get out in time. I remember when I was young, we had to go stay with Aunt Myra many times." She patted my shoulder.

Finally, Uncle Luke pulled up in front of the house in his

big blue van.

I ran to open the door. The wind slammed it against the wall. Bolts of lightning shot across the sky. Thunder roared, and the house rattled. I eased between the door and the wall to wait for Uncle Luke. He was a very big man, and the wind was pushing him.

"This is a bad one! At least the rain has stopped for now," he shouted over the roaring wind.

Uncle Luke finished putting the suitcases and the cooler in the van. "You two go back inside and wait for me to call you when I'm ready! I have to board up the windows and put out sand bags. It'll only take an hour or so. Glad I started getting those planks and sand bags ready a few days ago when I came by. Had a feeling the storm would come. Just didn't think it'd be this soon. Or this bad."

I stood inside the door to watch him. He leaned into the wind, pushing his way to the garage to get the planks to cover the windows.

"Lil' Portia!" He called for me to come outside. "Hand me those nails out of that can."

The wind lashed around us as I handed Uncle Luke the nails and he hammered the planks to each window frame. I had to stand against the wall so the wind wouldn't toss me about.

Three of Grandma's neighbors saw Uncle Luke working

and came over to help.

"The wind is so strong, and we need to hurry and leave. The rain will soon start coming down again." one man said. "We'll help so we can *all* get out before it's too late."

When they finished, Uncle Luke said, "Thank you for your help. You were right. It would have taken me much longer. Take care."

Uncle Luke and I fought to get the nails, saw, and hammer back in the garage. I thought, if Dad were here, he'd help Uncle Luke.

"Okay, let's get going." Uncle Luke gestured toward the van. "We should be at Myra's in three or four hours." He squinted into the wind and shook his head.

We piled into the van. Mom sat in the front seat next to Uncle Luke. Grandma and I sat in back, with me behind Uncle Luke.

I wanted to read some of my books, but the wind made so much noise I couldn't concentrate.

I stole a glance at Grandma. She looked worried. The van shook.

"Do you think we'll run into a lot of traffic, Luke?" she asked her brother.

"We'll see when we get to the main highway."

On the highway, I could see miles and miles of cars, vans,

trucks, and buses. Police cars with flashing lights guided the vehicles.

"I've got to get in line somewhere," Uncle Luke said under his breath. Just as he finished speaking, a driver let the van pull in front of him.

"Remember, I said it'll probably take three or so hours?" Uncle Luke grunted. "Well, forget that. We'll be riding bumper to bumper for miles, and who knows when we'll get there. Good thing I filled old Betsy up yesterday."

Uncle Luke turned on the radio.

"The wind's growing stronger as Hurricane Kelly moves closer," the announcer said. "The sky has opened up and the rain is pouring down. We'll stay with you as long as we—No! We were just told to sign off. We have to evacuate too. Tune in to the emergency weather station for updates." The local radio station went out. Uncle Luke turned the radio off.

We rode for two hours in silence. The rain beat down on the van, and the wind howled. Grayish black clouds poured out gallons of water.

At last, we reached the highway leading to Greensburg County.

"I'm getting a snack. Anyone want anything?" I asked. When I got up to go to the back of the van, I fell against Grandma's seat. The van swayed. It felt like I was standing in the middle of a tugboat.

"Be careful and hold on so you won't fall, baby," Grandma said. "Your Uncle Luke removed the last seat so he could put his fishing and camping gear in the van."

"Old Betsy is my home away from home," Uncle Luke said, "when I want to get away to camp or fish. Need the extra space for a bed."

I held on and moved to the back of the van.

I opened my suitcase, got my kit, and tested. My blood sugar was low.

"Lil' Portia, bring me a bottle of water, please," Uncle Luke called.

Mom looked over her shoulder. "Me too."

When I'd finished making my sandwich and grabbing one of Grandma's homemade gingerbread cookies, I gave each of them a bottle of water.

"How much longer to Aunt Myra's?" I asked Uncle Luke while munching my sandwich, eyeing my cookies.

"Well, if we keep on moving like this, we should be there in about three more hours."

"At least we're out of the worst part of the storm. I see a little sunlight up ahead behind the clouds," Mom chimed in.

Grandma looked back. "Goodness gracious! Nothing but darkness," she mumbled. "I'm afraid this might be one of the worst hurricanes we've had in years. I pray that all the neighbors made it out in time."

Traffic began thinning out.

"We'll make good time now," Uncle Luke said.

We drove through many small towns. This part of the state had a lot of farms and very few people. I remembered coming through these towns over the past years going to visit Aunt Myra. Mom would drive, and Grandma would sit next to her. I always sat in the back seat, looking out the window, counting houses and cars, trying to catch a glimpse of different farm animals.

This trip was different. We had to make it to a safe place.

For a second I closed my eyes.

Screeeeech! Screeeeech!

My eyes popped opened just in time to see a big yellow truck skidding toward my side of the van.

"Look out! Truck, Uncle—"

In a flash, the truck smashed into the van. Boooom! The windows shattered. Something sharp hit my arm. Ouch! I looked down and saw blood. My head and shoulder hurt. I couldn't feel the rest of my body. The van slid sideways shaking and rolling from side to side, but that whale-of-a-van didn't turn over. It landed in the ditch with a loud thump.

"Portia! Portia! Are you all right?"

I opened my mouth to speak, but no sound came out.

Chapter Seventeen

"Portia," a soft voice called. "Are you awake?"

I cracked open my eyes. My left arm hurt. There was a white cast on it.

Mom leaned in close to my face.

"What happened?" I rasped. My throat felt so dry that it hurt to swallow, and my head throbbed. "Where am I?"

"You're in the hospital, baby," Mom whispered. "The doctor said the worst part is over, and it's only a matter of time before you'll be ready to go home."

I sniffed. My nose felt like it was stuffed with cotton. "When can I go home?"

"The doctor hasn't said yet. We were waiting for you to wake up from the surgery." Mom took a seat on the side of the bed.

"Why am I here?" I asked.

"We were in a terrible accident, and you blacked out. The doctor had to make sure you didn't have any severe damage to your head. You had surgery to set your broken arm. There were small cuts on the left side of your body from the glass. Some glass had to be removed." Mom gently rubbed my right hand. "Uncle Luke got a whiplash, and his left shoulder was hurt. Nothing happened to me, but some flying glass cut Momma's hand. She had to have a few stitches."

I slid closer to Mom.

She hugged me. "We've been so worried. Uncle Luke and Momma are waiting outside and can't wait to see you. I'll go get them." She gave me a kiss and rushed out to bring them in.

Grandma had a small bandage on her hand. Uncle Luke had a big brace around his neck and a blue sling on his left arm. When they saw me, grins flooded their faces.

I forced a half-smile and waved my good hand. Grandma moved close to the bed. "We're so glad you're awake. Many prayers were sent up for you."

Uncle Luke leaned over and patted my head. "I love you, my Lil' Portia Grace. You take good care of yourself, you hear? I'll go so you can talk with your grandmother. I'm going to take your mom with me to get something to eat. She wouldn't leave your side until you woke up." He motioned to Mom, and she smiled and followed him out of the room.

Grandma walked over and gave me a long kiss on the cheek.

She carefully eased down on the hospital bed and put her arm around me.

"It was a horrible accident." She frowned. "Luke tried to avoid the truck, but …" She threw up both hands. "But the truck just shot through that intersection too fast and slammed into Luke's van."

"I'm glad you're here, Grandma."

She wrapped her arm back around my shoulders. "The truck completely totaled the van. Luke said if we'd been in a car, we'd all have been killed!" She shook her head. "The driver said the sun was in his eyes. The highway patrol is looking into the accident."

"It's good that Uncle Luke had that big monster of a van."

Grandma rubbed my face and smiled. "Yes, we always teased him about how big and ugly it looked, but it held up through this storm. And saved our lives."

"Why did only me and Uncle Luke get hurt bad?

"You and Luke were sitting on the side where the truck smashed into the van straight on. I'm glad you're all right. We saw blood, and we didn't know what was wrong. You didn't even make a sound." She squeezed my hand.

I didn't ever want her to let go.

"I'm glad all of us are okay." I squirmed in the bed trying to get comfortable before I asked quietly, "Does Daddy know?"

"Yes, your mom called him as soon as the doctors finished examining her. He flew here yesterday to see you and to make sure we were all right."

"Is he here?" I couldn't wait to see him. I watched the door, hoping he'd walk in.

"He had to go back home last night, but he'll be back early Friday morning to pick up you and your mom from Myra's. See those beautiful flowers?" Grandma pointed to the round table by the window. "He brought them for you, and he also delivered some good news. Dr. Thomas has ordered you an insulin pump. I know you remember what that is. When you get back home, you and your mom can learn how to use it. No more shots!"

"That's great." I closed my eyes and tried to make myself feel happy.

"You don't sound so excited about not having to give yourself anymore shots. You've got something else on your mind."

"I'm worried about Mom and Dad, Grandma. Will Daddy ever come back to live with us?" I opened my eyes and looked at her.

"I'll let your parents discuss that with you when your dad gets back. They agreed that they would talk to you at Myra's house when you got out of the hospital. They need to tell you themselves, honey."

I looked deep into her eyes. "Do you know if Daddy is coming back?"

Grandma just smiled. "Your dad will be here Friday morning." She gently put her cheek against mine, knowing that this was all the medicine I needed from her.

The next day I was released from the hospital, but I would have to wear the cast for a month or more. Mom made sure I stayed in bed, rested, and kept my arm raised. I could only get up to use the bathroom and eat.

I took my diary out of the suitcase.

Dear Diary,

We were in an awful accident. I can't remember very much of what happened. This cast makes it hard for me to roll over in bed. It's not easy sleeping in Aunt Myra's bed, but it's better than being in the hospital. Mom says I have to be still and not move about so much. At least I can move my right hand.

Daddy will be here early Friday to pick us up, and he and Mom will talk to me. I'm so excited and nervous. How can I wait one more day? I hope he's coming back home! I miss him so much.

—Hopeful

Mom let me come to the kitchen to eat my afternoon snack. They were all sitting at the kitchen table talking and eating too.

"It'll be at least a week before we can go home to see what damage the hurricane has done," said Uncle Luke, looking out the window. "Finally got through to the Public Works Department. Said to call back the first of next week. Electricity will be back on then."

"You're all welcome to stay here as long as you need to," Aunt Myra said. "I'm glad to be of help and to have your good company."

"Thank you, Myra. We know we can always depend on you," Grandma told her. "But I know Portia and Grace are ready to go home. Someone has a birthday coming up soon."

"I'm excited about my birthday," I said, brushing the bread crumbs from my lips. Mom smiled and handed me a napkin. My birthday was not that important now. I was impatient to find out what news Mom and Dad had for me.

Since Grandma wouldn't tell me, was it bad news?

Chapter Eighteen

Thursday—I watched the clock all day. I can't remember anything that happened. All I thought about was Mom and Dad talking to me—and Friday. Was Dad coming home? Would everything be all right? That night, I tossed and turned and hardly slept at all.

At last, the morning sun. I sat up in bed to listen for sounds or voices from the kitchen—*none*. Where was Daddy? Isn't he coming home? Now I know why Grandma didn't tell me. They're getting a divorce! My eyes started to tear up.

But then, I heard loud voices, talking and laughing from the kitchen. And I heard *his* voice.

"Daddy's here!" the words rang in my head. "He's here!"

I hummed while I quickly washed up. I checked out my face in the mirror. No big scars. I gave myself my shot, crossed my fingers for good news, and rushed to the kitchen. Everyone sat around Aunt Myra's table drinking coffee and eating biscuits and ham. I couldn't even think about eating food, but it smelled good, so good.

"Hey, Baby Girl!" Dad rushed towards me, putting his arms out.

"Hi, Daddy." I ran to him, and he held me tight.

"It's been a long time since we've been together," Dad said holding me tight. "When I saw you in that hospital bed, I was worried." He shook his head. "I wanted to pick you up and take you home and make all the hurt go away. I missed you and your mom so much."

I eased down in the chair next to him. My arm in the cast hurt a little. Aunt Myra put a glass of milk and a warm buttered biscuit in front of me. "Eat, baby." She smiled at me.

Uncle Luke picked up his coffee cup, and he and Aunt Myra left the kitchen.

Now the news. My heart skipped a beat. My heart skipped two beats.

"Portia, I know it's been hard for you." Dad frowned. "You've grown up so much this past year since you turned eleven and had to take full responsibility for your diabetes. Now it's time to tell you about the problem we've been having." He shifted in his chair. "Mom, Grandma, and I love you more than life itself." He took both my hands in his. The cast felt like it weighed a thousand pounds. "We're asking you to understand one more thing." He stopped.

I heard him swallow. "Daddy, what is it? You're scaring me." My voice quivered and my hands started to sweat.

"When I was in college, I had a girlfriend." Dad's voice was serious. He stared down at our hands. "We wanted to get married. Her father thought we were too young and he didn't really like me much."

Oh, no! Dad was in love with someone else. Was he going to marry someone else like Mary Ann's dad?

"Six months before I graduated, we got married anyway."

I looked at Mom. She stared down at the floor.

"After I finished college, I couldn't find a job, so I joined the Air Force. I had to go away for basic training. Two months after I left, my wife's dad became ill. She went back home to take care of him and to finish college there. Six months later, she sent me divorce papers and asked me to sign them."

Dad stopped talking and wrinkled his forehead.

"Then what happened, Daddy?"

"I tried to talk her out of getting a divorce, but she said she'd given it a lot of thought, and her father was right—we were too young for marriage and she wanted out."

Was Dad still married?

"After agonizing over the situation, I signed the papers and sent them back to her. I was sure her dad had a lot to do with her decision."

Dad was not married to someone else. So what was the problem?

"Three years later, I got out of the Air Force. I met your mom, we fell in love, got married, and the next year you were born. I was so happy."

Mom's eyes met mine and she smiled.

"About two years ago, I received a letter telling me I had a daughter from my first marriage. I couldn't believe it. Why did she wait so long to tell me?"

My stomach cramped into a ball. Dad has another daughter!

"I got in touch with my ex-wife to ask her about our daughter. I found out her name is Jasmine and she had been asking about me. Her mom finally decided it was time to tell me. She said she'd been debating for years if she should tell me. I was furious. I kept the letter and didn't mention it to your mom until last year." Dad looked at Mom. "I realized that it was wrong keeping it from her. I wanted to see my other daughter, and I wanted her to know us." He turned to me. "Your mom and I talked, but we never could agree on what to do. The pain made it hard for us to be nice to each other. That's when we decided to separate to sort things out."

Again, Dad turned to Mom. "I never meant to hurt her. Your mother was upset because I didn't tell her when I received the letter. I should've told her the minute I got it, but I was so angry and wasn't sure what to do." Dad glanced back at me and rubbed my fingers.

The room went silent.

My mind raced, trying to find an answer to our problem. I remembered Mary Ann's sad blue eyes after her parents' divorce.

My whole body ached. I didn't want that to happen to me. I sniffed back tears. "I still want you to come home, Daddy."

More silence. Grandma cleared her throat.

What should we do? I looked at Grandma. My stomach lurched.

Her eyes met mine. She answered my unasked questions. "Portia, I won't give my opinion because it's not up to me. Your mom and dad made their decision on their own."

"But, Grandma—"

"We've talked and this is our decision," Mom cut in firmly. "We're a family and I love your dad. We won't live apart any longer." She shrugged and looked right at me. "This happened long before we met. There is more than enough love in this family to welcome another daughter. I want your dad home, too."

I jumped up. "Yes! I'm so ready for you to come home, Daddy!"

Dad smiled and leaned over and gave Mom a long kiss. Then Mom and Dad stood up and held out their arms, and I leaped between them. My cast almost hit Dad and he pretended to duck.

Grandma, Dad, and Mom laughed so loud that Uncle Luke and Aunt Myra rushed into the kitchen. Laughter and joy filled the Maddox family once again.

That afternoon, Mom, Dad, and I left Grandma and Uncle Luke at Aunt Myra's house. It would be a week before they could go back home. Hurricane Kelly did a lot of damage, but their houses were not destroyed.

We were going home, Dad, Mom, and me.

The plane glided across the bright, clear, moonlit sky. The storm had passed. Mom and Dad, holding hands and sitting next to me, made me realize how important my family is.

I would be twelve years old in two weeks. I never thought I'd get my dad back home and a half-sister for my birthday.

The Monday after we got home, Mom called Dr. Thomas for an appointment so we could begin training with my new insulin pump.

Two days later, Dad called Mom and me into the kitchen. "Hey, ladies, come look at this." He lifted the lid off a shoebox in front of him. "Baby Girl, come sit next to me. I want to show you some pictures of your sister, Jasmine. She sent them to me early last year. I think you two look alike." He smiled at me. "Your mom has seen the pictures already. She thinks Jasmine and you look alike too."

I could feel Mom's eyes on me as I looked at each picture.

"She has the same hazel eyes as you and your dad." Mom spoke in a soft voice, then smiled at Dad.

"How old is Jasmine?" The name felt strange and unfamiliar on my tongue.

"She's sixteen," Dad replied.

"Oh boy, she's old. When can I meet her?"

"Your mom and I decided that you and I would go for a visit this summer, after your cast comes off. How do you feel about that?"

"I'd like that. I want to see her." I stroked the smooth cast on my arm nervously. "Suppose she doesn't like me?"

"I think you two will get along fine," Dad said. "I've been talking to her on the phone for a few months now, and you have lots of things in common. One of them is very important—she loves jewelry too." He winked at me and laughed.

"Oh, Daddy, you're so silly." I laughed back.

My birthday was on a Sunday this year. Grandma sent me a birthday card with money in it.

"Do you want a party, dear?" Mom asked.

"No, I am so happy that Dad's home and we're going to

California. And besides, I have this old cast and it's a pain having it on."

"My, Portia, you are growing up. How about we take you out to eat at that new fancy restaurant, Bocelli's, downtown," Mom said. "Would you like that?"

"Yes! That would be great. I can wear my new green dress and gold necklace. Good idea. I love you, Mom."

The last day of August, the cast came off, and Dad and I made plans for our trip. He was going to rent a car so we could go sightseeing. We made reservations at a hotel not far from Jasmine's house. Jasmine and me would share a room. I was excited and nervous.

The night before the trip, Grandma called. "Yes, Mom, she's so thrilled," I overheard Mom on the phone. "Russell said he was going to take them to Disneyland. You can only imagine how much she is looking forward to this trip. Her bags have been packed for days." Mom laughed quietly. "Portia, Grandma wants to talk to you."

I took the phone from Mom and turned around. "Hi, Grandma."

"Are you ready to meet your sister?"

"I'm a little scared, but I want to meet her."

"I don't think you have anything to worry about, just be you. If Jasmine is anything like Russell and you, she has a good spirit. She's probably more nervous about meeting you. She doesn't know your dad either. Portia, it's your job to make her feel at ease and welcome her into the family. You can do it, baby. Okay? Remember, you've had a father all these years. She hasn't. I love you. Come back and tell me all about your adventure. Tell your dad to enjoy this special trip."

"Thank you, Grandma. I love you too." Grandma always made me feel special.

Just before going to bed that night, I wrote,

Dear Diary,

I don't want anyone to know, but I'm nervous. Grandma knows the right thing to say to me. I'll try to relax and be myself. We are both dad's daughters. Dad and I will fly to California to meet Jasmine tomorrow. I have a million questions jumping in my head. What will I say to her when we meet? Will she like me? Does she have diabetes? Will Dad call her "Baby Girl" too? That's what he called her on the phone. No, he'll have to give her another name! That's his name for me. How does Mom feel about Jasmine? Will she accept her into our family and ask her to come for a visit sometimes? Grandma said I have to take the lead.

Butterflies are dancing in my stomach again. Not knowing what might happen on this trip, I'm scared.
—Off to Another Adventure

I closed the diary and opened my suitcase to make sure I had packed the necklace for Jasmine.

Is Portia out of the storm?

ELP BOOKS®
California

Acknowledgments

To my children, who continually inspire me: Tanja, Don Jr., Darlene, Tayonna, and Dejah. To my family, who have always believed in me. To my friends, who constantly encourage me.

This book would still be a dream if not for the support of Southwest Manuscripters writers, and friends. Special thanks to South Bay Writers Workshop—Nina, Donna, Joyce, Jody, Edith (deceased), Bob B., Dale, and Bob C.—you challenged me to soar. My appreciation to The Society of Children's Book Writers and Illustrators, which made the Redondo Beach Writers possible. I will forever be grateful to members of this group for your relentless editing and feedback— Devi, Mary Jo, Lia, and Karen—you made me believe that I could do it!

My gratitude to Bernadene H. Coleman, Shelly Howland, Darlene Loiler, Elaine Mirsky, Barbara Vogel, Geralyn Goodman, Mary Burnette, Kathy Oh, Katje Lehrman, Claudine Phillips, Tanja Aldridge, Janik Sundher and Linda Maher for showing me that a simple idea could become a living, breathing children's story.

Thank you, Frank Zanca, for your time, your advice, your technical publishing knowledge, and support at the finish line.

Many thanks to Gail Jackson-Bassett and her fifth graders at Castle Heights Elementary School in Los Angeles, California, for inviting me to "share" my book. Your enthusiasm ignited my writing spirit.

Without the encouragement of colleagues, friends, and loved ones, I could not have completed this journey. I owe all of you a huge debt of gratitude. I am so thankful for each of you who walked this journey with me.